DEATH TO A TENOR

DEATH TO A TENOR

FRED MacISAAC

POPULAR PUBLICATIONS · 2021

TABLE OF CONTENTS

DEATH TO A TENOR

He Sang in Darkness as a Publicity
Gag—but Black Mystery Shrouds Him
and the Horrible Riddle of His Murder
Whitens Peter Hunter's Hair

1

THE SINGER IN THE DARK

I'M A PERSON you read about but rarely meet, a man whose hair turned white overnight. I'm a prosy, humdrum sort of fellow by the name of Peter Hunter, owner of the Hunter Advertising Agency, which came out of the ruck into the big money through Ronald Ray, the radio star. Circumstances pushed me in the middle of the Ronnie Ray mystery. I'm no daring adventurer, no Argus-eyed detective; just a good business booster.

I'm used to the white hair that came from a night of horror; but I still have bad dreams and wake up trembling, my snow-white locks standing on end, to find myself in my own bed and not in the abominable inn where I saw the grisly spectacle. Point is, I had as much to do with the Ray case as the police or the Federal officers; more, maybe.

Sure—the way to tell a story is to begin at the beginning. This one begins with the debut of a radio singer named Ronald Ray. Ronnie had a marvelous voice, of course, but he came in the middle of the crooner craze, and what put him over was showmanship.

Now, Ray had no manager—nobody to put him wise to the wrinkles which attract the public—and he did not give the impression of having so much on the ball mentally. It looked like his natural shyness was responsible for the stunt that made him the biggest star on the air.

He told me, the first time I talked with him, that it was an accident. He had a job in a vaudeville theater, a big combination house, and when he walked out on the stage he found himself in front of a microphone for the first time.

He went dumb with fright, but his accompanist rushed into the wings, had the stage and house lights turned out, dashed back to the piano, and started his accompaniment. After that he went over like a house afire.

I never checked up on this story, mind you. Every stunt starts more or less by accident, but when I first heard of Ronnie he was singing on a sustaining hour at International—the I.B.C.

He was billed as the Singer in the Dark, and carried out the idea by working in a small studio with the lights out. Whether he sang in darkness or light didn't matter to the radio audience, of course, but you'd be surprised what

"What's up there?"
Kittie called

*I turned my
flashlight through
the open door*

silly tricks are pulled in broadcasting studios to impress
the staff.

At International Broadcasting there are a score of
studios, ranging from the auditorium, which seats two
thousand spectators and where a broadcast may be a
symphony concert or a stage show in which the radio
actors wear costumes, grease paint, and such, to a small
room like a parlor with no provision for an audience and
nobody present save the man at the sound control board
and the announcer.

The small studios are mostly for sustaining programs.
A sustaining program is intended to prevent a moment's
silence during the many hours of operation of a great
broadcasting station. The artists are usually singers, pianists,
violinists, and lecturers who are trying to break into radio.
They stand round waiting for something to happen to a

regular, highly paid and sponsored program. The sustainers
fill in the gaps in the sponsors, a sponsor being a commercial advertiser. The business of the radio station is to get rid
of sustaining programs as rapidly as they can sell the time.

Ronnie Ray began work at International in one of these
tiny studios, with the lights out. His accompanist could
play in the dark, of course. Most good pianists can play
with their eyes closed. I've even seen one of them lay a
sheet over the keyboard and give a swell performance of
a complicated number that way. Lita Lawton, the accompanist, was one grand pianist.

I WAS RESPONSIBLE for "Perfumes of Arcady" grabbing
Ronald Ray. It was Kittie Ketchum, my secretary, who put
me onto him. In those days Perfumes of Arcady was a small
concern owned by a queer looking little French-Swiss who
had begun by manufacturing the perfumes personally in
the kitchen of his flat in New York. His business had grown
so that he could afford a small advertising appropriation.

As mine was a small agency which gratefully accepted
chicken feed, I got the account and had begun to do fairly
well with it.

"Pete," said Kittie when she came in one morning after
being out sick the day before, "I tuned in the radio yesterday about eleven-thirty and picked up a coot named
Ronald Ray."

"You're five minutes late," I said sharply. "And you've a
day's work piled up there. Make motions."

Kittie made a face at me. Time was when Kittie hadn't
got paid regularly, and yours truly hadn't eaten regularly—
in the early days of the agency—so I put up with a lot from
that Tenth Avenue harp.

"He did funny things to me," she said as she seated herself. "Made my spine quiver and put a lump in my throat and tears in my eyes. It's the strangest voice I ever heard, Pete. Not like any crooner. Better. Soft and sweet and rich and dear. Made me wish I'd been a good girl all my life."

"Bushwah," I retorted. "Take fifteen or twenty letters. You're too darned good. I've scars to prove it."

"And the queer thing is," she said, "that my room seemed to fill with exquisite perfume while that lovely voice drifted through the air."

"The girl is nuts," I remarked to my inkwell.

"So, said I to myself," she continued, "Ronald Ray is exactly what the doctor ordered for Perfumes of Arcady."

"Swartz, Rosenbaum and Ikeburg," I dictated. "Dear sirs—"

"Pete, listen to me! He's on a sustaining program. He can be had cheap. Make Duplon buy fifteen minutes on some station."

"Shut up and take dictation."

"Okay, dunderhead," she said angrily.

About half an hour afterwards the door opened and in came Pierre Duplon—Perfumes of Arcady accompanied by his fat wife. Pierre was a small, shriveled, dark, gnome-like man with a bright light in his black eyes. Madame would have made three of him.

Pierre looked sullen and angry, and madame looked eager.

"*Mon ami,*" began Pierre, "ma femme, she is crazy."

"*Zut,*" replied madame. "Without me, Claire Duplon, where would you be? Monsieur Peter Hunter, is it expensive, this radio?"

"Plenty," I replied.

"*Voilà!* It is as I said," declared Pierre.

"It makes no matter," replied madame. "Yesterday I hear a *diseur*, a *chanteur*—"

"Madame," screamed Kittie Ketchum, "you heard Ronald Ray!"

"*Mais oui, mais oui!*" screamed the big woman.

Instantly the pair were in each other's arms, crying on each other's shoulders, while Duplon and I looked at each other in astonishment.

"Screwy," I said. "Balmy."

"*Vraiment,*" replied the Swiss-Frenchman. "Without doubt."

"But if it affects both of them like that," I said, "you and I will make a call immediately upon the broadcasting station."

"If you do not get him," cried Madame Duplon, "never return, Pierre, to the *chez* Duplon!"

Well, in this radio business everything is ratty. Ronald Ray was the most marvelous thing that had ever cooed into a mike, but practically nobody of importance at the studio had found time to listen to his initial broadcast. There was the sound engineer, of course, but those guys get so they hear automatically.

Jones, who was on duty with Ronald Ray, was so sore because Ronnie insisted on turning out the lights that he would have considered him rotten if he had been the late lamented Caruso.

So International didn't know what they had, and they sold Ronnie to Pierre for almost nothing and gave us a punk spot in the afternoon for a reasonable figure. In an

hour we were back and
displayed our contract to
Madame Duplon.

NOW, THAT'S THE
lowdown on the strange
start of Ronald Ray in
radio. Everything about
Ray was fantastic—his
finish the most of all. No
human being won fame
so fast, nobody was so
generally beloved and
so universally mourned.

Peter Hunter

Having been on the inside from the start, I am the only
person in a position to relate the whole weird, horrible tale.

I've got to begin at the beginning. If I seem to ramble
around, remember I'm an old newspaper reporter and I
know where I'm heading. Give me a break.

Perfumes of Arcady were "made" by Ronald Ray. In no
time at all people were stopping work in the middle of the
afternoon to tune in on him. He affected men almost as
much as he did women. Darn it, he had me weeping myself
and liking it!

His fees went up like a rocket. The little shop where
Perfumes of Arcady were manufactured grew into a
six-story building. In a year he was singing twice a week
at eight-thirty in the evening, the best spot on the program.
The Peter Hunter Agency moved into new and gorgeous
quarters. Madame Duplon was insanely in love with our
star. So was Kittie Ketchum, the hard-boiled little mick.
My only consolation about that was that Kittie had no

more chance than Madame Duplon. Kittie had a genius for organization that I lacked, and I needed her in my business.

Pierre Duplon had one grievance against Ronald Ray. He wanted to use the broadcast auditorium, fill it with two thousand people, and cash in on that angle of publicity. But Ronnie refused to budge from the little studio, and continued to sing with the lights out.

I argued with him and his accompanist.

"You don't have to play the Garbo of the Air any more," I said. "A radio star's life is short." How was I to know how short his was to be? "Cash in while you may."

I argued with Miss Lawton, the accompanist, and she was as hard to budge as her boss—with the added inconvenience that she was dumb. I mean she couldn't talk. Something the matter with her vocal cords. I would give her a long argument, and she would write *No* on a piece of paper, and that would be that.

"Ronnie," I would say to him, "you're a big good looking blond bum, and you don't have to worry about making good in broad daylight. Grab these theatrical offers. They'll help Perfumes of Arcady. One for all and all for one. Hey?"

"No, Peter," he would say. "We are taking in five grand a week, and that's plenty. Twice a week is as much singing as I want to do. I don't mind being led around like a prize bull if it's good for our business. I'll go to cocktail parties and suppers and let them turn the spotlight on me and make a bow, but Miss Lawton doesn't care to make theatrical tours, and she's sensitive about appearing in public on account of her dumbness. I can't get over my nervousness about singing before a crowd, and if I see a mike I'm sunk."

Pierre Duplon was always blowing off because Ronnie

wouldn't let him bring the world to the broadcasts, and Madame Duplon grieved because Ronnie refused to permit anybody to be present, not even his sponsors, upon Perfume Nights. However, we were all getting rich the way things were, so we made the best of it.

Kittie Ketchum

At the end of the second year my agency had more business than it could attend to. Ronnie was getting ten thousand a week. Perfumes of Arcady had made millions and was outselling French perfumes in France. We had Ronnie hard and fast except for tilting the ante every six months. The way the cash was rolling in, that didn't worry us in the slightest.

And along came Barbara Bond.

Barbara Bond was about the richest girl in the world and one of the prettiest.

2

YOUNG LOVE

SHE WAS TWENTY-ONE years old. She was a yachts-
woman and an aviatrix, and the national champion
outboard motorist. Her pictures were in all the Sunday
papers all the time. Being an advertising man who understood all the tricks of the photographer's trade, pictures had
always left me cold. I'd never seen a really beautiful woman
aviatrix or champion outboard motorist, but when Kittie
Ketchum, who arranged all my appointments, led Barbara
Bond into my office, I was as dazzled as though a bolt of
lightning had exploded right in the room.

Now, Kittie is no mean dish herself. She is a cute little
trick with chestnut hair and fine brown eyes and a sort
of monkey grin and a very neat figure. When she first
joined my staff—she had been the staff in those days—she
was just out of business school, and her speech smacked
slightly of "dese, dem and dose," but she had sloughed off
all that. As my office manager, she was dignity and elegance
personified.

Barbara Bond, however, was something unique. She was
the blondest blonde that ever came under my observation.
She had vast eyes of sea blue. Her skin was snow and rose.
Her teeth were small, matched, glittering pearls. She was

slender but not thin, willowy and lithe and yet deliciously feminine. She wore a simple little blue costume, but that girl didn't need clothes. She was above and beyond them. She brought in with her a radiance. I seemed to see gold rays darting from her. In short, she sunk me.

"This is a pleasure, Mr. Hunter," she said. The voice finished the job. There was a ringing in my ears and goose-flesh took possession of my body.

"Snap out of it," said Kittie coldly. "This young lady is here on business."

I looked upon Kittie with venom. "Leave us, please," I said in a voice that wasn't as steady as I would have liked. "Please sit down, Miss Bond."

The delectable young lady sank gracefully into a chair and smiled upon me devastatingly.

Here was a girl whose grandfather had been a Pennsylvania coal miner, and whose father had been a hard-bitten miner who had been hated cordially by his hundred thousand workmen and all business associates. And she looked like the daughter of a long line of aristocrats.

"I need your help," she said. "I want to meet Ronnie Ray."

Some of the glamour of her faded. Just a woman, like Mrs. Duplon and Kittie and everybody else.

"I've written him," she said, "and I've called his suite and left my name, and I've even tried to speak to him in the street. I'm told that you can arrange a meeting."

Well, a girl like that was out of my class. While I was only thirty-one and better looking than Ronald Ray, in my opinion, I can't sing sweet songs in perfumed tones, and the female sex is gaga anyway.

"I'll throw a party at my diggings," I said. "Ronnie will come and I'll introduce you."

"Wonderful," she said. "What I really want is to have him sing at a party in my house on Fifth Avenue, which I am reopening."

"Not a chance. He never sings outside the studio."

She thrust out her little chin.

"That, of course, is a pose. I'll make it worth while for him to change his attitude. I'll pay him one hundred thousand dollars to sing one song, and I'll pay you ten thousand to persuade him to do it."

I sucked in my breath. One hundred grand!

Ten grand for yours truly!

I'd knock his block off if he didn't accept.

"I'm seeing him this afternoon," I said. "I'll put it over. It's about time he snapped out of it."

"You're a remarkable man," she said enthusiastically. "When shall I know?"

"I've an apartment on Madison at Sixty-seventh Street," I said. "I'll have people in at six this evening. Ronnie will be there. Would you like to come?"

She leaped to her feet, laughing gleefully.

"Oh, you darling!" she cried. "May I kiss you?"

I lifted up both hands.

"You'd ruin me for life," I protested. "You're too gol-darned beautiful."

With a laugh she threw her arms around my neck and pressed her soft, warm lips to mine. The blood rushed up to my brain and out again as the door opened.

Kittie Ketchum gazed upon us.

"Mr. Duplon is waiting," said Kittie in a tone which conveyed volumes to me.

Miss Bond laughed and turned to Kittie.

"I'm leaving. Mr. Hunter has done me a wonderful favor, and I'm so grateful."

"So I see," said Kittie dryly.

Barbara Bond

"Good-by," said Barbara in a voice that would melt gold.

"Good-by," I murmured. Like a dying calf, I guess.

She went out, and Kittie came over to me.

"You poor, pitiful poached egg," she said scornfully. "Do you suppose she would be annoyed with you? She's after Ronnie."

"Sure she is," I agreed. "And I'm having her meet him at my apartment tonight."

"I'll be there myself," stated Kittie. "That girl is so perfect I'd like to assassinate her. It's not fair."

"And she wants Ronnie to sing at her house for one hundred grand. We get ten for putting the deal across."

Kittie became businesslike. "Will he, do you think?"

"He will, or I'll beat his head in."

"You'd do a lot for that Barbara Bond, wouldn't you?"

"And for ten grand. Everything added to what you've got makes just a little bit more."

"Well, I'll bring in Duplon," Kittie said.

He had nothing important to say, and soon left.

RONNIE OCCUPIED A suite at the Ritz, and when I arrived there he was finishing a rehearsal of a new song with Miss Lawton. I had to wait in the next room. There was something uncanny about the effect of his voice. It was a light baritone with amazing sweetness and infinite appeal. There was none of the gobbling and whispering of crooners. This fellow was a great singer whose tones were peculiarly suited to the idiosyncrasies of the air.

In a couple of minutes he opened the door. The accompanist was putting some manuscripts into a briefcase. She nodded and smiled at me. Her smile was peculiar. There was no sweetness in it, and no smile in her black, expressionless eyes. Her teeth were good, but they didn't make up for the commonplace aspect of her face. She was an old maid type, and probably would have been a seamstress if she hadn't been a musician. Ronnie had informed me that she was a marvelous coach and he couldn't get along without her.

"Listen, genius," I said. "There comes a time in the affairs of men when it's necessary to grab. How would you like to grab a hundred thousand dollars in one large lump?"

"Why, fine," he said. His speaking voice was pleasant but not unusual. "Whom do I kill?"

"Nobody. Miss Barbara Bond wants you to sing one song at a private party. I know your attitude, but here's where you change it."

He glanced at Miss Lawton. She shook her head.

"It's a temptation," he said regretfully. "But nothing doing."

"Ronnie—"

"Nope. I'll pick up a hundred grand in a few months anyway. And I've got lots of dough. Tell her to save her money."

"Tell her yourself. I'm giving a cocktail party at six. She'll be there."

He shrugged his shoulders. "Another one of those dames," he remarked. He grinned

Ronnie Ray

at the accompanist, and she smiled back.

"Barbara Bond is not another one," I said. "She's the loveliest thing that ever breathed, Ronnie. You've behaved very well for a radio singer, but you'll fall for this one."

"Women worry me. Make me uncomfortable. I won't go to your party."

Miss Lawton nodded to me, picked up her brief-case and left the room.

"How the deuce can she coach you when she's dumb?" I demanded.

"Her fingers aren't dumb. She can make the piano sing a song exactly as I'm supposed to do it. I've seen this Bond girl's picture. She's something better than pretty nice!"

"I'm asking you to turn up as a favor. Frankly, I'm hipped on her. You'll have to turn her down personally. I can't. She—well—she kissed me when I said I'd bring you."

Ronnie slapped me on the shoulder. "You old rascal," he said. "Well, as a favor to you I'll show up."

For a musician he was a pretty decent chap. In two years he had behaved himself, kept out of woman trouble, never missed an engagement, did no drinking, and had positively not acquired a swelled head. His popularity was growing instead of waning. According to International checkups and the receipts of Perfumes of Arcady, everybody in America, Europe, and Australia, not to mention Asia and Africa, tuned in on him.

The strange part of it was that Ronald was a very ordinary sort of chap who had been born in uptown New York, sold newspapers, worked in a shoe store, had not been to college and was entitled to have his head completely turned.

By not trying to cash in on every prospect that came along he was prolonging his radio career. He was blond and had nice, straight features and a slow, pleasant smile. Certainly not a fellow who needed to sing in the dark. I had a notion that his fear of the mike and of spectators was a bluff. With his experience he would have gotten over his initial timidity long ago. However, it was a swell act.

WELL, I THREW the party and invited a dozen people. Barbara came at six sharp, arriving with Kittie. The Duplons came five minutes later with a couple of fellows from my office and a team of actresses from a Harris show.

At six-thirty Ronnie strolled into the room and everything grew tense. Barbara was standing beside the piano turning the pages for one of the actresses, who was playing. She turned and looked at him and he gazed at her.

I saw his eyes, and knew that Ronnie Ray, the Galahad, had arrived at the end of his rope.

The women all crowded around him. Kittie introduced

Barbara. After a minute the other women drifted off forlornly, and Barbara and Ronnie went over and sat on a couch in a corner.

Kittie took my arm and smiled up at me.

"You're Paddy-the-next-best-thing," she said. "Ronnie has gone out of my life."

"Humph! Was he ever in it?"

She giggled. "Not that he was aware of, but for two years I've been hugging my pillow at night wishing it were he."

"You give me a profound pain," I said huffily.

Kittie laughed. "Look at them!" she said. "Well, we're both brokenhearted."

"Say, do you suppose I'd be fool enough to fall for the richest girl in America?"

"You'd be a fool if you didn't," she replied." She's lovely, lovely."

By and by Ronnie and Barbara came to me arm in arm.

"If you don't mind," she said, "we're going out to dinner."

"Bless you, my children," I said. "How about the proposition, Ronnie?"

"I'm singing at Miss Bond's party," he said, with an infatuated, foolish smile.

So the champion aviatrix, outboard motorist, and what not, had proved to be the champion woman of America. After they left, the party broke up by unanimous consent.

The following morning a crisp check for ten thousand dollars turned up in an envelope addressed to me. At ten o'clock Ronnie called me.

"Peter," he said, "I'm engaged to be married to Barbara Bond."

"Well, you could do worse, but I don't know how," I said.

What the heck? I knew that I never did have a chance with a girl like that.

I didn't hear from him after that until the next evening, and then I did not hear directly.

A woman called me on the phone at my flat one hour before the time of the broadcast.

"I'm speaking for Miss Lawton, Mr. Ray's accompanist," she said. "She wants to know if you know where Ronnie is."

"I haven't seen him."

"Well, he usually rehearses before the broadcast, and he is not at his suite. Miss Lawton is worried."

"Tell her to stay right there. I'll call Miss Bond's house."

I didn't expect Barbara to be home, but she was; and came immediately to the phone.

"Is Ronnie with you?" I asked anxiously.

"Of course not. He's broadcasting. That's why I'm home. He won't let me go to the studio."

"When did you see him last?"

"About one o'clock this morning. Why?"

"Well, his accompanist had someone telephone that he hasn't got in touch with her. She is very much worried."

I heard Miss Bond gasp, "What do you suppose has happened?"

"I've no idea. I'm getting to the studio right away."

"I'm coming too," she cried. "Oh, do you suppose anything has happened to him?"

"Certainly not. He hasn't missed a broadcast in two years. He'll turn up."

"Just the same, I'm coming.

She hung up. I grabbed my hat and coat, rushed out of

the apartment, hailed a taxi—and was driven to International.

3

WHERE IS RONALD RAY?

ON RONALD RAY nights they had special policemen outside the place to keep back the crowd, special cops inside to watch the elevators, and guards posted in the corridor leading to Studio Five, in which he worked.

This had become necessary because every possible trick to get into the studio had been worked by every sort of person from prominent company executives and wealthy sponsors down to ordinary gate-crashers. I had to show my credentials to reach the entrance to Studio Five, and there I was stopped short.

Bishop, the announcer, came out to see me; looking very worried.

"Miss Lawton is inside," he said. "He hasn't shown."

"We've half an hour yet. Wait a minute."

I saw Barbara at the end of the corridor arguing with a guard. I went down and fetched her.

"What does Miss Lawton say?" I demanded when I returned.

"Nothing, of course. This is what she has just written down."

He handed me a slip of paper from the pad the dumb woman used:

Ronnie didn't call me today, and didn't appear at his suite for rehearsals. I presume that everything is all right and that he has been spending all his time with his fiancée.

I showed it to Barbara. "Did he seem all right?" I asked her.

She smiled anxiously. "We had a lovely evening and he seemed very happy when we parted at one this morning. He was going to call me when he waked, and I've been home all day, but I haven't heard from him."

We stood there waiting hopefully until it was ten minutes before broadcast time, when Miss Lawton came out. As the broadcasts were private, she never dressed particularly for them, and upon this occasion she wore a black crape costume which revealed the scrawniness of her figure.

She scribbled something on her pad and handed me the slip.

I'm afraid something has happened to him.

Barbara put out her hand and with a slight hesitation the accompanist took it and smiled. She appeared to be overawed by the effulgent beauty of the girl.

"I'm so happy to meet you," said Barbara sincerely. "Ronnie says that you are perfectly wonderful, and that he couldn't possibly get along without you."

Miss Lawton wrote on her pad.

Thank you. The question is, what has happened to him?

Suddenly Barbara burst into tears. She turned to me and laid her head against my chest and sobbed like a child.

Miss Lawton turned away.

The announcer looked at his watch.

"Five minutes more," he said. "I'll have to talk against time. He is sure to come. He's never been late before. The world is waiting for him at eight-thirty. I'll have to talk about him—soothe them. Don't worry. I'll hold his audience."

The tribe of announcers are all alike. Conceited little fellows, most of them, deluded with the notion that listeners enjoy their silly long-winded announcements.

This fellow imagined he could say something which would interest and hold people who wanted Ronnie's golden voice.

The production manager, a hale, bluff, hearty fellow, appeared suddenly on the scene.

"This is a catastrophe," he said tensely. "Where the devil is the fellow? He was the one man who could absolutely be depended upon, and now he falls down on us."

"Be still, you idiot!" cried Barbara. "Something awful must have happened to Ronnie."

He turned upon her indignantly, met her marvelous eyes, and crumpled.

"You're Miss Bond, of course. I beg your pardon. Of course there has been an accident."

"Oooh!" cried Barbara. "There has been an accident!"

She turned again to me and her tears soaked into my shoulder.

It came to be eight-forty-five, and the Perfumes of Arcady period was over. After two minutes an electrical transcription of a Ray broadcast had been turned on. Ronnie did not come.

He was never to be seen again in a broadcasting studio, but of course, at the time, we did not know that.

I took Barbara home and offered to keep her company, but she insisted that she wanted to be alone. So I went disconsolately off to my flat.

Just as I entered Kittie called up.

"What happened?" she demanded.

"He didn't show up, that's all. Maybe he's been in an accident. He certainly wouldn't go off on a drunk like a lot of these hams."

"Get busy," she snapped. "He's been kidnaped."

"How do you know?" I exclaimed excitedly.

"I don't, but he must have been! Why, he's a bright shining mark, the biggest personality in America, and just engaged to the richest girl. Oh, why didn't he have body-guards and everything!"

"I'm going to phone all the hospitals and the police," I told her. "I don't take any stock in kidnaping. After all, he isn't a rich man as they go."

"Idiot, the people of America would raise a million ransom for him!" she cried hysterically. "They love him. They can't get along without him. I'm coming right over."

"Come along," I said drearily. "Maybe you're right. In that case we have a lot of work cut out for us."

THE NEXT WEEK was a nightmare. Police, detectives, nuts with notions, false clues and mountains of mail. Ronald Ray had disappeared off the face of the earth. We used a second electrical transcription, and then we learned that people could not bear to hear the voice of their vanished idol.

We had four weeks more to run on our old contract with International, and we were fighting a stiff raise in our broadcasting charges when Ronnie disappeared.

I scurried round to find a new star, but the Duplons got cold feet. Madame told her husband that nobody could replace Ronnie, and it was foolish to continue advertising Perfumes of Arcady over the air. I told him it was suicide not to, but he canceled and pretty soon found out that I was right.

Ronnie had left Barbara Bond's house on Fifth Avenue to walk to the Ritz Hotel that night. He had never arrived there. Nobody had recognized him, nobody appeared to explain what had become of him.

Perfumes of Arcady offered fifty thousand dollars reward for his safe return. Barbara Bond announced through the newspapers that she would pay any price. Despite police protests, we broadcast to the kidnapers that we would pay what they demanded, and implored them to communicate with Miss Bond, or to the office of Peter Hunter and Company. Nothing came of it.

Of course the hue and cry was enough to terrify any kidnaper. The Federal government offered its services to the New York police. Every newspaper man in America was on the job. Volunteers by the hundreds of thousands were combing the countryside all over the nation, examining deserted houses, crawling into caves, and climbing mountains.

No news.

Perfumes were by far the biggest account in my office,

and Perfumes were at present dead. Duplon's sales were falling off and as his revenue shrunk, his audacity shrunk with it. I couldn't persuade him even to advertise in newspapers.

Miss Lawton was offered a large sum by a tabloid to write her recollections of Ronald Ray, and refused. Barbara Bond shut herself up in her home and would see none of her friends.

Waiting... waiting....

A cousin of Ray's came in to see me after Ronnie had been gone a week. He was a shifty-eyed, shabby little man who was accompanied by a shyster lawyer who called himself Samuels. The cousin's name was Ralph Ray, and he lived in Hackensack. "We want to know about Ronald's estate," the lawyer said. "Mr. Ray here is the only heir, so far as we know."

"Ronnie isn't dead yet," I said sharply. "And the kidnapers will be paid whatever they ask, so your client's chances of inheriting are very slight."

"That's all right," said Samuels, spreading out his hands palms up. "What we'd like to know is, where is his money?"

"In the bank, I suppose."

"I have ways of finding out things," said Samuels. "He has checking accounts in two banks, and they amount to only six thousand dollars. Will you tell me how much money he has earned since he broke into radio?"

"Well, pretty close to seven hundred thousand dollars."

I thought that Ralph Ray was going to faint.

"What did he do with it?" the lawyer inquired.

"Invested it, I suppose."

"I happen to know that he has no deposit box at either

of the banks in which he deposits funds, and no securities were found by the police in his suite at the hotel," Samuels went on.

"Well, I haven't got his money. We paid him by check, and what he did with the cash is his own business," I answered.

"Yes, but it's queer there's nothing visible. He would deposit your checks, and within a day or two draw almost all the money out in cash."

"That is queer," I said thoughtfully. "I can tell you that he lived quietly, was supporting no woman, and making no expensive presents. I never heard of his buying stocks or real estate. I suppose the police know what you're telling me."

Samuels grinned. "Sure. I got a pull at headquarters."

"What's your theory?"

"Blackmail," said Samuels. "Somebody was blackmailing him."

"I think the people who were blackmailing him kidnaped him," said the cousin. "Find the blackmailer and you got the kidnaper."

"Now, my friend, let me show you how you're wrong," I cut in. "The kidnaping stopped his income. The reason the kidnapers haven't been heard from is that it's an extremely difficult job to arrange to pay over a large sum of money to snatchers. We are willing, but the police are watching. It was much more simple to keep on blackmailing Ronnie. In another year they'd collect half a million."

"That's right," said Samuels. "Pay no attention to Ralph. He don't know anything."

"I don't believe he was being blackmailed," I said

thoughtfully. "Ronnie was no mental giant. Maybe he was hoarding. Most likely he has his cash tucked away in a vault in a bank in which he hasn't a checking account. I don't believe the boy spent more than two or three hundred dollars a week. Look here. I can't tell you anything. Go and see Miss Lawton, his accompanist. She was entirely in his confidence. They were together for years."

"We've been to see her," confessed Samuels. "She says like you do, that he's alive and it's none of our business. Besides, she's dumb."

4

THE DOVER ROAD

"WELL, SORRY I can't help you gentlemen," I said to end the interview.

They left and I had something to think about. Understand that my position was advertising agent for Perfumes of Arcady, Ronald Ray's sponsor. The police didn't tell me what steps they were taking and what they were finding out, if anything. I was vitally interested in the return of Ronald because my business needed him, just as much as Duplon's Perfumes needed him; but I was sitting in my office working every day to mend my fences.

My spare time was being occupied listening to radio programs trying to find a good number to sell to Duplon. Kittie was spending a lot of her evenings with Barbara. Those two girls were as different as day and night, but they had cottoned to each other. Barbara clung to Kittie, and Kittie claimed Barbara was as lovely in her character as her appearance.

Three weeks had gone by, and nothing had happened. I was sitting in my apartment listening to the radio at eleven on a Saturday night. I was feeling gloomy. Duplon's cowardly attitude was putting my business on the bum.

I'd heard a dozen stars who would do Perfumes of

Arcady good—not Ronald Rays, but worth carrying on with—and the confounded little Swiss had turned them all down. Broadcasting that night was particularly horrible. At eleven five my doorbell tinkled.

I opened. Kittie.

Kittie's eyes were gleaming and her face was white and she was shaking.

"Ronnie," she exclaimed. "He's been heard from!"

"Glory hallelujah!" I yelled.

She lifted her hand. "Not yet. Half an hour ago Barbara heard from the kidnapers. She's been in communication with them secretly—"

"Why didn't you tell me?"

"Because she didn't even tell me. She has two hundred thousand in cash ready to pay over to them, and she's been waiting for the word. Half an hour ago she got it."

I leaped from my chair. "Well, well!" I cried jubilantly.

"She's gone," Kittie went on excitedly. "She had to go alone and make sure she wouldn't be followed."

"With the money?"

"Of course! She is to be met outside Dover, New Jersey."

I reached for the phone. Kittie grasped it from my hand.

"No, no!" she cried. "She told me in confidence. I wanted to go with her, but she was told she must be alone. She left in her roadster, and I grabbed a taxi here."

"That's a lonely place up near the lake region," I said. "A good hideout for kidnapers, though. The police ought to follow her."

"They warned her, I tell you! If she disobeys instructions Ronnie will be k-k-killed."

"But that girl, alone in that country? With two hundred thousand in cash!"

"We'll follow her," Kittie decided. "Get your car. Hurry."

I hesitated.

"Haven't you any guts?" asked Kittie scornfully.

"Come on," I snapped. "I'll show you."

FIVE MINUTES LATER we rolled out of the garage in the new cabriolet I had bought a few months back when I supposed that Ronald Ray would go on forever. We fretted at delays caused by traffic lights but we made good time to the Holland Tunnel, and I stepped on it when we reached the Jersey side. The way to Dover leads through Montclair. In an incredibly short time I was in Montclair, but I didn't flatter myself that I had gained on a girl who was a speed demon in the air, on the water, and on the road, and who was carrying the ransom for the man she loved.

It began to rain when we left Montclair. The season was early April and the rain was cold and a raw wind was blowing. We did very little talking during that ride, I remember. The road was narrow and despite the windshield wiper, visibility was poor.

Barbara, Kittie said, was driving a brand-new speedster with the curious air-flow shape that was comparatively new on the road. She had explained over the telephone to the kidnaper that her car could easily be recognized for that reason.

At a gas station in Dover we learned that such a car had passed through forty-five minutes ahead of us.

"Did it stop?" I demanded.

"No, it went flying through. I just noticed it on account of the funny radiator."

I thanked the attendant—and noted that Barbara had gained on us. We drove through the main street of Dover. The wind had risen, and the rain beat heavily against the windshield. Torrents.

"Hurry up," Kittie kept saying. I drove faster than was reasonable.

Some miles beyond the road forked. I turned instinctively to the right, signs being invisible. Kittie didn't even notice the fork. After a time I began to have misgivings. The road became rougher and narrower. It was almost impossible to see ahead, but we were in a wooded country.

I don't suppose I was doing more than twenty-five when I crashed into a barrier. The wheel was jerked from my hands, the right side of the car sank into a deep ditch and we went over, with a rending and shrieking and roaring of the motor.

Kittie made no sound as we overturned. Plucky little Irish girl. I bumped my head so hard against the windshield that I pretty near went unconscious. I heard her groan and realized that I was laying on top of her, that the car was on its side in the ditch, and the motor was making sinister sounds. I reached for the switch, found it and turned it off. I succeeded in bracing my feet against the right hand door and lifted my weight from Kittie.

"Badly hurt?" I asked anxiously.

"Bunged-up but serviceable," she came back. "It's lucky you're soft from lack of exercise or you'd have broken some of my bones. How about getting out of this?"

I was trying to get the door, which had become the top of the car, open. After some effort I succeeded. I managed to climb out and lifted Kittie out.

"A lot of help you are to Barbara!" she commented. "Well, I've the use of my arms and legs, and that's something. What struck us?"

I WENT FORWARD. A sizable tree had fallen across the road. We had crashed into it, bounced, and toppled into the ditch. A wrecking car could right my bus. I couldn't. The rain was blinding and bitter cold. Kittie was wearing a light woolen coat.

I went round to the rear of the car, succeeded in getting the hatch open and pulled out a raccoon coat, always there for emergencies, which she accepted gratefully.

"I'm afraid we can't do anything for Barbara," I said. "At first I thought the kidnapers had blocked the road, but that tree blew down."

"By the looks of the road," she said tartly, "Barbara would have known better than come down it. It's a side road. What now, Pete?"

"Shelter," I said curtly. "It must be about fifteen miles back to Dover. Maybe there's a village nearer in the other direction."

"I didn't notice any between here and Dover. Fifteen miles is a five-hour walk under decent conditions, and I've slippers on."

"Any sort of house will do. We'll wake some of these countrymen up," I said cheerfully. "There must be a house within a half mile or so."

I secured a flashlight from the side pocket of the car, took her arm and we stepped over the tree and trudged along.

"I'm sorry I let you in for this," I said mournfully. "I should have come alone."

Kittie laughed lightly and squeezed my arm.

"You let me in! I forced you to come. And you couldn't have left me behind."

We said no more because the rain was beating into our faces. There were holes full of water in the road and speedily we had our feet soaked. For five minutes we trudged along, when suddenly and unexpectedly there came a flash of lightning which made everything clear as day. Crossing the road ahead, strung on very tall poles, were high-voltage electric wires, and directly ahead we saw a large sheet of water, a lake.

And to the left were several buildings.

"A break!" I exclaimed. "At least we can get out of the rain."

We broke into a run and presently arrived on the porch of a place which obviously had been an inn—one of the many small wayside inns one finds in that section. It was boarded up, of course, as were several outbuildings, including a gas station.

"There will be a fireplace inside," I told her. "And we can burn some of these window boards and get warm." I peeled off my coat and began to pry at the boardings. Despite Kittie's gibe at my softness, I have powerful muscles. The nails came out easily. In a few minutes I had a window exposed. Picking up a stone I broke a pane completely out and was able to thrust my hand inside. The window, however, was not bolted. I pushed it up, climbed in and helped Kittie through.

"Well," she said, "I'm compromised. We'll have to stay here all night, since you seem to have picked a road that nobody else would think of using at this time of year."

"We'll have to stay until the rain stops," I answered. "If there's a phone here, it's sure to be disconnected."

I swung the flash round and discovered the fireplace. There were dry logs, kindlings and a fire all ready to be lighted. In a corner of the room was a grand piano with a green cloth covering. At the far side was a small hotel desk, and beyond a flight of stairs.

"Piece of luck," I said. "Beds upstairs. We won't do so badly."

Kittie suddenly began to cry.

"I'm thinking of Barbara," she sobbed. "Suppose something happens to her!"

I set about making the fire, there being no answer to her remark. I had tried and I had failed and Barbara was in the hands of the gods. In a few minutes I had a good fire going, which illuminated the room with a ruddy glow. The warmth was grateful and we both warmed our hands over the blaze. I pulled up an English settle in front of the fire and settled Kittie there.

"I will now go up and see about sleeping accommodations," I told her peremptorily.

"If you can't find two rooms, forget to come back," she retorted.

I walked to the staircase—and became aware of a strong and very unpleasant odor. It was worse than the mustiness of a little hotel boarded-up for months. It was strange and indescribable.

"Maybe they forgot the cat," I muttered as I forced myself to go up the stairs. I arrived in a broad hallway, on one side of which were six bedroom doors. One of these stood open.

The smell was stronger. Holding my nose, I forced myself to the open door and turned my flashlight within. The sight I saw I'll never forget. How can I? It still appears in horrible nightmares.

5

THE DEAD THING

THERE WAS A man sitting in a chair, strapped in. His head hung forward on his breast. His two hands were clutching a thick wire. He was in an advanced state of putrefaction.

I would have fled, but the hair, the shape of the head, the greenish-brown tweeds the dead man wore, caused me to stiffen as though I, like him, had been electrocuted. This wretched human being had been sitting there for weeks, dead and decaying.

And I knew who it was. Ronald Ray, the radio star.

Something stronger than myself forced me to walk up to the body. I dared to unbutton the coat. I thrust my hand into the breast pocket and drew forth a wallet and a letter. The letter was in a feminine hand, and the address was: *Ronald Ray, Ritz Hotel, New York.*

The wallet was empty, but contained two of his visiting cards. I replaced them in the pocket and staggered out of the room. I felt my knees buckling; my eyes failing and things going black. The air was full of poison, but the horror in my heart was more dreadful.

I reached the top step, staggered, collapsed, and arrived at the bottom without being aware of it.

I came back to life with my head in Kittie's lap. My

collar had been loosened and she was rubbing my hands and sobbing.

"Have you been upstairs?" I gasped.

"No. I—I didn't dare. What's up there? Why did you faint?"

"Nothing alive," I said faintly. "Don't go up."

"I won't. Pete, is somebody dead up there?"

I was able to nod my head.

She shuddered. "I don't mind the rain," she said. "Let's get out of this dreadful place."

I sat up. The horror was still on me but I had to get the girl out of there. I'd already displayed shameful weakness.

Kittie eagerly helped me to my feet. She helped me on with my coat. By that time my strength had returned. I couldn't tell her what I knew. I mustn't tell her.

We got out through the window and faced the driving rain with more determination than before. After a few minutes, she asked timidly:

"There was a dreadful smell. Had it been there long?"

"Yes. Let's not talk about it. I've got to report it."

"Makes you sick to think about it. I didn't see it, and I'm sick."

We tramped along. Presently we came around a bend in the road and saw a small headlight in the distance. We hurried our steps. The headlight was upon a motorcycle with sidecar. It was stopped beside our overturned bus and a State trooper was inspecting it with a flashlight. I shouted to him.

He jumped into his machine and ran down to us.

"Were you two in that car?" he demanded.

"Yes," I said. "Is there a house near here where you can put this girl? I've something important to report."

"What is it?"

"How far away is this house?"

"About a half mile back."

"Put her in your rumble seat and get her quartered, please. I'll wait until you return."

He flashed the light in my face and seemed satisfied, for he helped Kittie into the machine.

As I waited beside my overturned car in the rain, a phase of the situation which had not occurred to me presented itself. Ronnie was dead, had been dead for weeks. He had been assassinated in a most horrible manner—coldly, deliberately, after elaborate preparations.

It was more like an execution than a murder. In fact, he had died in an electric chair. And that indicated vengeance—the vengeance of a madman for some real or fancied wrong.

But it also meant that he had not been kidnaped for ransom. He had been slain immediately, or within a day or two after his disappearance. By whom? Why? Certainly not by commercial snatchers of persons of prominence.

And that meant that those who had demanded two hundred thousand dollars of Barbara Bond were not the kidnapers—they were outside criminals attempting to cash in on a situation! Something like that had occurred in the Lindbergh case. She would deliver the money—but she would not get back her fiancé. Perhaps she might be held by the snatchers, slain, or a demand made for her safe return!

WAS IT A coincidence that she had been ordered to proceed

in a direction which led Kittie and me to the body of Ronald Ray? Or was it the original kidnapers of Ronnie, who might have a hide-out in this thinly settled section of New Jersey?

I didn't know. I couldn't think very clearly. What I had seen was before me at this minute. I began to shake, but snapped out of it when the motorcycle headlight came into view.

"Put her to bed at Mrs. Waterson's," said the trooper. "She went all to pieces, poor kid. Now what's on your mind, fellow?"

"In that inn down the road," I said, "you'll find the body of Ronald Ray, the kidnaped radio star."

He swore and his hand closed tightly on my shoulder.

"And how do you happen to know whose body it is?" he demanded.

"Because I'm the head of Hunter and Company, advertising agents, for whom Ronnie was working on the radio," I replied.

"You can prove that, I suppose."

"Certainly."

"That inn is boarded up. Sort of queer you get in there and find this fellow, eh?"

I pointed to the car. "We ran for shelter. Got in through a window, lighted a fire and I went up to see about bedrooms. He—he was electrocuted, officer, deliberately. The broken-off wire is still in his hands. He's been dead for weeks."

"Get into the side car," he said. "We'll have a look-see. How come you happen to be in this country on a night like this?"

"We were following Barbara Bond, Ronnie's fiancée

who is taking two hundred grand to men who claim to be the kidnapers."

"Down this way?" he demanded excitedly.

"I think we got off the main road."

"You did that, all right."

We drew up at the inn and he dismounted.

"Come on in," he commanded.

"Couldn't I stay outside?" I pleaded.

He shook his head. "You get through that window ahead of me."

For the second time that night I entered through that window. The fire, of course, was still blazing. We hadn't stopped to extinguish it in our flight.

"Come on," he said impatiently.

I folded my arms. "Shoot me if you like. I'm not going up those stairs again."

"Humph! What you got to identify you?"

I produced my wallet, cards and several letters which he inspected.

"All right, stay here," he said gruffly. He went up the stairs two steps at a time. In half a minute he came down, white and shaking.

"I never saw anything like that," he muttered. "My God, have you got a drink?"

"If I had a flask I'd have emptied it."

"I almost fainted," he said candidly "Say, the face is gone. How do you know it's him?"

"By the hair, the shape of the head, the suit he's wearing and a letter in his pocket from Barbara Bond, the girl we followed out here."

The cop managed a grin. "I'm taking your word for that,"

he said. "If you touched that thing you've more guts than I have. Not if they broke me would I lay hands on it. Come on. Let's you and me get into Dover and report."

As we departed from the accursed place the trooper said:

"He won't never sing any more. Say, my wife listened to him regular! I did myself when I was home. He made you feel good, that fellow. Whoever done that to him ought to be boiled in oil."

"At least he died quickly," I muttered.

"Yeah, but think of being made to sit down and getting strapped in and taking hold of the wire. That girl didn't see him?"

"No, thank God! She doesn't even know who it is. He was a friend of hers, too."

I GOT INTO the side car and he drove the motorcycle at sickening speed back to Dover, where we entered the police station and he reported what he had found at the inn to the astonished and horrified cop on duty. Later he phoned state police headquarters from a booth. He talked for fifteen minutes while I sat in the office. I was cold and shivering and miserable.

"Don't do for an old man like you to be out in the wet," said the local cop sympathetically.

"What do you mean, old man?" I asked indignantly.

"Well," he retorted, "you're a gray haired guy, ain't you?"

"I am not!" I shouted.

"Take a squint into the mirror."

He thumbed to a mirror over the washstand. I got up and looked at myself and had to grab the washbowl to keep from fainting. My hair was white. And my face was lined and haggard and my eyes were wild. But the hair! I ran my hand through it. It felt the same.

I staggered back to my chair. I'd heard of people turning white during their sleep, but I hadn't been asleep. I've asked a lot of doctors about it, and you can have their explanations; they don't make sense to me. I guess it started to turn when I touched the body of Ronnie Ray.

By and by the trooper came out of the booth.

"Sergeant Murphy is on his way," he said. "Word is to hold you till he gets here. Can you give this guy some dry clothes, officer?"

The Dover cop nodded. "Sure. We can fix him up."

"Say," I said hysterically, "my hair was black when I went into that place. It's turned white."

The trooper stared, touched his own hair and ran to the mirror. He sighed with relief.

"Okay," he said, "but I ain't going back. I'll resign first."

"Come on feller," said the local policeman. "I'll put you in a nice clean cell, and give you a change of clothes and dry these for you. Maybe you can get some sleep."

"I got orders to go out after this Barbara Bond," said the trooper. "Back in an hour or two, maybe."

I felt a little better in dry clothes and lay down on the cot, but I couldn't close an eye. While I'm not vain, I hope, it was a horrible blow to find that I had white hair thirty years too soon. And if I fell asleep I knew what I'd dream about. So I stayed awake."

Along about six A.M. the state trooper was back. He came into the cell and offered me a cigarette.

"I've been clean to the Pennsylvania line," he reported. "No trace of her. Funny thing, though. At a railroad crossing about ten miles up, the gates were down and had been smashed through on both sides. Big, thick timbers knocked into kindling wood. They had no business being down. Nobody on duty after ten o'clock, on account of no trains coming through. Kind of funny."

"Isn't it?" I said absently. I was wondering if I could dye my hair back to its original color. Queer that a thing of that sort seemed so important, considering what had happened during the night.

Just then Sergeant Murphy came in. He was a middle-aged, iron-jawed fellow with gimlet eyes, and he questioned me and the trooper at length.

"Some connection between the murderers of Ray," he said, "and the crooks who brought Miss Bond out this way. I don't believe in coincidences. They must have made a hookup with the high voltage wires out at the lake to fry this crooner. That means one of them is an electrician. Well, Mr. Hunter, I'm going down to this inn. I'll have a wrecking car right your bus and bring it back if it will travel. How about this young lady who was with you?"

"Let her sleep until eight o'clock anyway. I'm comfortable here. She had a shock too," I replied. "Are we free to go?"

"Sure. You're credentials are okay. We have your identification of the body. You got any notion why they should carry off this poor guy and electrocute him?"

"Certainly not!"

"Don't make sense. Criminals work for profit like everybody else. No profit in killing a man worth a king's ransom."

"Of course not."

"I'd say these crooks who communicated with Miss

Bond were outsiders if they hadn't set the rendezvous near where the murder was committed," the sergeant added.

I had no comment to make.

Murphy grinned. "My wife was nuts about this singer. Maybe some woman's husband got fed up with her ravings and went out to put an end to the guy."

I had to grin. "No doubt a good many husbands would have liked to, but I don't think that's the solution."

Murphy rose. "Come on, Fields," he said to the trooper. "We have things to do."

6

DEMON DRIVER

KITTIE AND I drove my battered car into New York. I dropped her at her apartment and went directly to the office. Kittie was in a state because I had had to tell her who was dead upstairs at the inn. And she was shocked almost as badly at the sight of my snow-white hair.

"It's becoming, though, Pete," she assured me. "I don't know if it doesn't make you look better—more distinguished—"

"I was satisfied the way things were," I said mournfully.

It was nine-thirty when I entered my office. The staff, of course, were knocked speechless at the change in my appearance. I told them briefly how and why and that finished them. No doubt a number felt it spelled the loss of their jobs. I'd held my people, hoping that our income property, Ronnie Ray, would come back to us. They figured that Hunter and Co. wouldn't be as big an agency in the future as it had been before Ronnie was taken away.

"Mr. Hunter," said the phone operator, "Miss Bond wishes to call you as soon as you came in."

"What?" I shouted. "Get her quick!"

In a moment Barbara came on the line.

"I've had the most dreadful experience, Peter," she began.

"I'm hopping right up to your place. Hold everything," I cried excitedly.

In ten minutes I jumped out of a taxi and rang the bell at the Bond house. The butler was expecting me and led me into the study and Barbara came in within a minute. She wore a blue street dress and she looked spic and span and as fresh as if she had had ten hours' sleep.

"Thank God nothing happened to you!" I exclaimed, taking both her hands.

She smiled. "I knew Kittie would tell you about my trip and that you would try to stop me. It was useless, Peter."

"I know it," I said dolefully. I had to tell her. How could I tell her what it was obvious she didn't yet know?

Barbara sat down. She lighted a cigarette. Her eyes snapped.

"I was victimized," she said. "I knew, of course, that there was a possibility that the persons in communication with me were not Ronnie's kidnapers, but I had to take the risk, hadn't I?"

"I suppose so."

"I've had the cash ready for some time, according to instructions. The word came last night. Kittie wanted to go with me but I was told to go alone. Besides, if this was a trap, I didn't want the child endangered."

"She's as old as you are."

Barbara smiled her brilliant smile. "Well, I'm hard. I've had every sort of experience and it was my fiancé who was in the hands of criminals. My instructions were to draw up at a gas station just beyond Dover, New Jersey. I followed them. When I arrived there, a black sedan was waiting. A man came from it and told me that I was to follow that

*"Got you!" said this hood
through clenched teeth*

car, keeping several hundred yards in the rear, but not to lose sight of its tail-light. I agreed and he got into the car, which immediately started off."

"Weren't you frightened?" I asked.

"Certainly I was frightened. I'm used to doing things that frighten me. I was alert for treachery and I had a gun in my car. I'm an excellent shot."

"You're an amazing person."

"Thanks. The car started out at a very fast clip, but of course I had no trouble following. It was raining terrifically and there was thunder and lightning occasionally and the road was greasy. I never lost sight of the tail-light, though. Ten miles out of Dover we were both doing sixty and I wondered why they were driving so fast. At that pace, of course, the headlights are of little use in case of trouble as it's impossible to stop in time if they reveal an obstruction. However, I didn't worry about things like that. I was thinking of Ronnie."

I turned my face away because it might betray me.

"We passed a big lake on the right and a few miles further along there came a terrific lightning flash which illuminated everything like daylight.

"I SAW THE car I was following some three hundred yards ahead, but half way between us was a railroad crossing, which the other car had passed. The gates had been lowered! And standing at the right of the road were three men.

"Everything was black in a second, but I knew then that I had been deceived. I would be forced to stop by the closed gates, and the three in the road would rob me."

I was so moved I couldn't speak.

"In a fraction of a second I made my decision," Barbara said. "My headlights were already lighting the gates. I could stop if I threw on the brakes immediately. Well, I stepped on the gas. I guess I hit those gates at eighty miles an hour. The good old car smashed them into smithereens. First one and then the other. My fenders were crumpled and my headlights went out, but I threw on the side lights and got a little vision. I went tearing after the decoy car—"

"Weren't you hurt?"

"Bumped a bit, but the shock wasn't very terrible. I had my gun and I intended to catch that car and fire into it. Well, the tail-light vanished. I think they heard the crash, ran into a side road and turned out the lights. Anyway I didn't overtake it. After a while I slowed to a safe speed, considering the weakness of my lights, and presently I came into Delaware Water Gap and put up for the night.

I cried myself to sleep, I was so disappointed. I wanted to bring Ronnie back."

"But they didn't get the two hundred thousand."

"Damn the money! What do I care about money?"

"I suppose you're the only girl in the world who would have dared to do what you did," I said worshipfully.

"Does that bring Ronnie back to me?"

The time had come. I gulped.

"What's the matter with you?" she said suddenly. "Am I mad, or is your hair white?"

"It's white," I said laconically.

Her eyes grew big as saucers. "I thought you looked queer, but I am so obsessed by my own affair—what has happened, Peter?"

"Barbara," my mouth was dry, I wet my lips, "it turned white last night. Kittie came to me and told me you had started with the ransom. We followed you—"

"But your hair—"

"We missed you, Barbara," I said pitifully, "but we found—Ronnie." She was on her feet. "What? Where? How?"

"Barbara, dear—he's—" I broke down and covered my face with my hands.

"He's dead," she whispered.

"He's been dead for weeks, Barbara."

Barbara dropped into a chair. "Oh, God!" she murmured.

"I think he was murdered directly after his disappearance."

"Then how could you find him? I don't understand."

"He died instantly—without pain—I believe."

We sat silent for a few moments.

"Why should anybody kill him—that dear, sweet, harmless boy?"

"I'm going to find out," I told her. "I don't care what happens to my business. I've got to find who did it."

"We'll find the murderer," she said firmly. "And punish him. I—I feel like a widow, Peter."

"Maybe I'd better go," I said nervously.

"No. Stay." She walked to a window, and stood there looking out. After a minute she turned slowly and came back.

"I'm all right," she said, smiling normally. "I can stand anything, I guess. You know, Pete, it was his voice I adored, but when I met him I stopped worshiping him and felt I ought to take charge of him. A maternal affection.

"He seemed to me as sort of bewildered, helpless, and needing somebody to guide him. Wasn't that a curious feeling for a man who had made a tremendous success in life? I'm sort of masculine, I guess, and he was almost feminine—I mean a real man, but with the weaknesses of a woman. I proposed to him myself. Well, I've something to live for, an object. Let's never let up. The police will lose interest. We won't. We'll run down this fiend, you and I."

She offered me her hand and I took it. Beautiful, dazzling, lovely as Barbara was, I felt at the moment as if I were shaking hands with a man. She certainly had the strength and courage of a man.

7

FEDERAL AGENT

THERE WAS A stranger waiting for me and talking to Kittie, who was at her desk looking a trifle pale, but efficient as usual.

"Mr. Hunter, this is Mr. Wright Forman," she said. "From the Department of Justice."

"Come right in," I said.

He took the chair beside my desk and lighted himself a cigar. He was a solidly-built person in his thirties, with sandy hair, a rather florid face and the coldest blue eyes I ever saw on a human being. He had a big chin, his lower jaw almost overshot. His hands and feet were big. His nose was squat and short, which gave him a long upper lip. He smiled—and that was the best thing about him. You felt sort of set up by his smile. When he spoke his voice was low and his speech was refined.

"Your secretary has related the events of last night," he said. "And I've the report of the New Jersey State police. Can you add anything to it?"

I shook my head. "And it makes me sick to think of that body in the homemade electric chair," I added.

"Well, let's start from somewhere else," he said. "You

were closely associated with Ronnie Ray. Can you give me a line on his friends and companions?"

"He didn't have any pals, so far as I knew. He was a queer fellow, Mr. Forman. I saw quite a little of him—I made him, you know. He kept decent hours. He never made whoopee. He was a retiring sort of bird and he never talked about himself. I've told the police all I know about him, and it didn't seem to help them much."

"The deduction was that this was a kidnaping job," replied the Federal man. "Inquiries were naturally along the lines suggested by that. It appears now that there was no ransom motive. They laid hands on him and immediately murdered him. The manner of the murder suggests revenge. It indicates that the killer seemed to think he was performing an execution. You realize it would have been much easier to stick a knife in him or riddle him with bullets than to hook up with high voltage wires? That's an exceedingly dangerous job."

"It's inexplicable!"

Forman smiled. "Nothing is inexplicable. I was wondering if, in the past, Ray had wronged somebody deeply. A seduction, perhaps—"

I laughed. "The poor devil wasn't that sort. If you had known him you'd laugh at the idea yourself."

Forman didn't smile. "Somebody hated him malignantly, hated him enough to arrange a horrible death for him. Our department goes through, Mr. Hunter. We never give up. We'll find the murderer among associates of his in the past—unless it happens that some maniac developed a homicidal hatred of his voice on the radio, which is not beyond the bounds of possibility."

"He was a singer, not a crooner," I said with a grin. "So I doubt that."

"What became of his money?"

"Oh, you've heard that it's supposed to have vanished?"

"I've been investigating this case two weeks," he replied. "I know he was accustomed to draw out his

Lita Lawton

salary checks, after collection, in cash."

"Then you've met the fellow who claims to be his heir?"

"Yes, I've talked with him. He's a worthless specimen, but hardly likely to do murder."

"Frankly, I never learned much about him. This Lawton woman, his accompanist, knows him better than anybody else. Talk with her."

"What do you suppose I've been doing with my time?" Forman answered. "I've had several interviews with her. She discovered his voice, trained him, made a contract with him by which she received ten per cent of his earnings—a reasonable commission considering that she was his teacher as well as his accompanist. She has lost her golden goose. A dumb pianist is not likely to be employed by another artist. A curious, pathetic creature, isn't she?"

"She struck me that way," I said.

He nodded. "I never saw a woman so completely at a loss. Evidently she took a tremendous pride at his success. She's worried sick about him, and doesn't know what to do with herself. It will be a shock when she learns of his death. The afternoon papers will carry it. In fact, extras are on the street now."

He rose. "I'll appreciate it if you'll get in touch with me if you run across anything helpful. I'm at the Great Northern Hotel."

"You know about Miss Bond?"

"I understand that she is safe at home. I'm on my way to see her."

"I've just broken the news to her, but I imagine she'll see you. She is feeling badly, but she's a strong, courageous girl."

"Yes, I know quite a little about Miss Bond," Forman said dryly. "Good morning."

HE WALKED BRISKLY out of the office and I picked up my mail and tried to get down to business. It wasn't possible. I couldn't get Ronnie out of my mind. Finally I pushed the letters away and lighted a cigarette and leaned back and began to think about things.

Find out who was bleeding Ronnie for his earnings and you pretty near had the murderer, I thought. Between the Federal and the state authorities they ought to find that out. Only why should anybody kill the goose that was laying the golden eggs?

Samuel, the lawyer of Ronnie's cousin and heir, Ralph Ray, said he must have been blackmailed. Well, suppose Ronnie had stiffened his backbone and refused to pay blackmail? They would threaten him and when he held out they might have carried him off. Maybe the execution flub-dub was to scare him. Maybe they didn't think the wire was charged and were as much surprised as the victim when it shocked him to death.

However, I couldn't see Ronnie in the role of a man who was being threatened. He hadn't impressed me as being of heroic stuff, and he certainly hadn't acted as though he was in terror of anybody. In fact, he was always very cheerful—considering that he was drawing cash out of the banks also as fast as he put it in and paying it over to blackmailers.

And when I had arrived at this point in my cogitations Miss Lawson was announced.

She wore a queer drab hat which almost covered one eye. She had on the shapeless black crepe dress she always wore in the daytime and often to the broadcasts. It was so old it was turning green. Her face was even more pale than usual. She had an old black silk umbrella, and the flat, square-toed black shoes she always wore stuck out beneath her skirt—which only came to her shoe tops.

I got her a chair and shook her hand sympathetically. It was a small but strong hand, and there were calluses on the sides of her fingers, like most pianists have. She smiled and sat down, and then she took her pad and pencil out of the handbag that hung from her left wrist.

"You know, of course," I began.

She nodded, scribbled on the pad, and handed me the slip:

> You and Kittie found him. It was very strange. Can't something be done to keep detectives from pestering me?

"I'm afraid not, Miss Lawton. You see, you were closest to him. You must tell them everything you know. All we can do for Ronnie is to make sure his murderer is punished and you might put them on the trail of the right one."

She shrugged her shoulders and wrote:

I've told everything I know over and over. I won't be questioned any more. There is a man named Forman, a terrible man. He treats me as though I were in some way responsible.

"He's a Federal detective, a very clever fellow. You want the murderer found, don't you?"
She wrote:

Of course, but I can't help. I'm having my mail sent to you. You have my permission to open it, if you like. I have no secrets. Later I'll send you a forwarding address.

"Are you going away?"
She nodded and wrote:

Yes. You've no idea how I am suffering. I found that boy. I taught him everything he knew. I must get where I can be left alone.

"Better tell me where you're going."
She shook her head decidedly and wrote:

I'll send you a forwarding address. Good-by.

I didn't think that the spinster would be allowed to disappear, but holding her was not my business. So I shook hands and let her go. As she was the chief clue to Ronnie's past I had a notion they'd consider her a material witness. I was right, but that woman disappeared off the face of the earth when she left my office. The idea that she would hide out on them apparently hadn't occurred to the police, or Forman either.

8

THE MAN IN THE TRAIN

I WENT TO lunch with Kittie and we talked the thing over and over. I told her how I had promised Barbara that I'd bring the murderer to book if the police didn't.

"You'd better attend to your own business, which isn't so good," Kittie said tartly. "Where do you get off solving murder mysteries? You're an advertising agent."

"Kittie, you know our financial condition when we ran across Ronnie. The money we've made we owe to him. And I don't think it was any accident that led us to that inn. We were drawn there by some Power, to make us realize the awfulness of the thing and to punish the murderer."

"You mean that you want to make good with Barbara Bond," she said sharply. "These horrible people, whoever they are, aren't going to be captured without fighting, Pete."

"I'm willing to fight—if I have to."

"I liked Ronnie. I mean I loved his voice," Kittie said. "Frankly, after I got to know him I wasn't infatuated with his personality. Anyway he's dead and the President has announced that all the resources of the nation would be set to work to capture the killer. That's good enough for me. Let's get back to the office."

When we returned Duplon, the owner of Perfumes of

Arcady and Ronnie's radio sponsor, was there waiting for me.

"Hunter," he said, "I got to sell the Perfumes of Arcady. You get me another big card and I will resume the programs."

"Just like that," I sneered. "You'll never get another Ronnie. We discovered him and picked him up for almost nothing. A chance like that comes once in a lifetime. Do you know what you've got to do? Buy one of the biggest stars of the air and pay through the nose."

"Who?"

"Well, I don't know who's available at the moment. A couple of weeks ago we could have had Bert Barton—"

"That crooner. Bah!"

"Will you get it through your head that there is only one Ronnie Ray in a generation?" I barked at him.

"I have talked it over with *la femme.* The wife says you find another or we do business with some other agency."

"Just like that! I made you and you ditch me," I said angrily.

"It was Claire, my wife, who discovered Ray not you, bluffer!" he came back. "I give you two weeks—"

With that the unreasonable French-Swiss turned and walked out of the office. Well, I had to save the account somehow. It was still our biggest asset. I called in Kittie.

"I've been listening for weeks," she said. "Nobody can follow Ronnie. Duplon's best bet is to use an entirely different kind of program. I've thought of a series of playlets, mysteries, perhaps, solved by the fact that somebody used Perfumes of Arcady."

"Get hold of all the radio agents and ask them for

their best bets," I contradicted. "You can't sell drama to Mrs. Ehiplon. We've got to get another singer. A woman, maybe."

Kittie smiled. "Mrs. Duplon hates women. However, I'll get on the phone."

The late afternoon papers practically discarded all news except the Ray murder. The reporters had dug up everything that the police knew and had done a lot of investigating on their own account. They had the life history of Ronnie, with a multitude of details that I never knew. They had found people who knew him at various ages—when he was a kid in the Bronx, when he worked in a shoe store on Sixth Avenue, when he solicited insurance for a big New York company.

Everybody agreed that he was a clean, exemplary young man. No one had been aware that he could sing, and all had followed his radio career with interest. The reporters found the manager of the Syracuse Theater, who remembered Ronnie's début and how his accompanist had rushed off stage when he stood frozen in front of his first microphone and, by signs, indicated that the lights be turned off.

There had been no women in his life. All who knew him agreed on that. And nothing in any way derogatory had been remembered by anybody.

From New Jersey came dispatches regarding the owner of the inn where the body was found. He was a man named Swartzman. He closed and boarded up his little hotel every October and reopened it the first of every June. He never went near the place during the closed period, running a lunchroom in Newark winters, which he turned over to a brother to operate during the summer season.

There were reports regarding the car which had tried to lure Barbara Bond to robbery and perhaps murder. It had been seen in a small town across the Pennsylvania line early in the morning, and then lost track of. They had a picture of me (secured from a photographer with whom I'd have a reckoning) and a lurid account of how Kittie and I had found the body. I didn't read much of that.

AT FIVE O'CLOCK I left the office and took the subway uptown. I live in a nice little apartment on West Seventy-fourth and always ride up on the subway express to Seventy-Second Street. I got off there as usual, and as I made for the stairs I happened to glance into a local train. The car was full of strap-hangers and as I looked a man who was holding a strap with one hand and reading a paper with the other glanced up.

I was frozen in my tracks. My white hair stood on end. I guess my eyes popped out of my head. I was petrified for a couple of seconds and the fellow's head disappeared behind his paper.

Then I gave a yell that made people hurrying past think I was crazy and plunged for the door of that car. Too late. The door slammed in my face and the train started.

"Stop it, stop it!" I shouted, grabbing the guard by the arm.

"Say, you're nuts," he growled. "Take the next one."

The train swept out of the station. And on board the train, holding onto a strap, reading a paper, was Ronald Ray, or his twin brother.

Cold sweat broke out on my forehead. I began to shake. What happened last night must have driven me crazy. How could Ronnie be in that car? He was dead. I'd touched his body. And yet this fellow was his replica. The same wide blue eyes, same wistful mouth—oh, I suppose everybody has at least one double. But with the chase for Ronnie in full swing for a month, how could this double have escaped discovery? Or had I seen a ghost?

You can't chase a subway train. You can't tell at what station anybody will get off. I'd had my glimpse, and that was the end of it. Well, my knees were so weak I had trouble climbing the stairs to the street. I took a taxi instead of walking home, and when I arrived in the apartment I threw myself on a couch.

Was it possible he wasn't dead? The body I had found wore his clothes, had his letters in its pocket. You don't have to see the face of somebody you know very well. A glance at the shape of the head identifies him. Ronnie was dead, all right. And this was some nonentity who happened to look like him.

That night I didn't feel like company. I dined in the cafe in the building and returned to the apartment. I turned on the radio. Mine is a very expensive set, capable of picking up stations in Europe and Japan, though the high-powered New York stations made this possible only when local broadcasting has stopped for the night.

At midnight I could get West Coast stations putting on their nine o'clock local programs. Finds are often made on the West Coast. For an hour I sat there switching from station to station, hoping to hear something or somebody who would fit into the Duplon program. To tell the truth, I don't care for most radio entertainment; and finally I turned off the machine.

I had been smoking like a furnace. The room was stuffy

and I opened the window—and jumped back as though I had been shot.

Ronald Ray was singing "Sweet Lotus Land," one of the Arcady hits. Oh, well somebody had an electric transcription. I located an open window across the court from which the song was coming and shut my window. It gave me the creeps to hear his voice.

It had to be an electrical transcription, because Ronnie had always refused to make phonograph records. He had lost a lot of money thereby. His reason was the same which caused him to broadcast in the dark. He couldn't sing into an instrument if he could see it. Thanks to the recording radio phonographs, however, there were probably thousands of electrical transcriptions of Ray songs in existence. But in view of the murder I didn't see how any admirer of his had the heart to set one going.

9

LOUIE THE LOUP

WELL, I'VE HAD to continue listening for talent. Duplon must be back on the air. I tuned in on a small station where amateurs are always being given opportunity to broadcast—and tuned right out, for a horrible soprano was assassinating an opera aria. And then I became aware that my doorbell was ringing.

I opened it and a man walked into the room. He kept his hat on. He was small and dark who, when he smiled, he showed very white, very even teeth.

"Mr. Hunter?" he asked in a soft voice. "I would like to talk with you."

I didn't like his looks, and I'd discussed the Ray case with enough detectives and investigators.

"Who the devil are you?" I asked sullenly. "A few words are all you're going to get."

"Now, my fren'," he said with another smile. "I won't detain you long."

He had on a tan topcoat, and he thrust his hand into the right side pocket. What warned me was that his black eyes narrowed to slits and his lips thinned to a narrow straight line. He tried to pull something from the pocket.

It appeared to catch on the lining and I kicked him swiftly in the groin.

He howled, doubled up and out came what he had in his pocket—an automatic pistol. Too late. I was on him and over him. Down he went, with me on top and both my hands grasping his wrist and the pistol. He let go of it, and I pasted him with all the force I could manage, considering that I was laying on his chest.

I ought to have grabbed the pistol, of course, but I wasn't using my head to think with. My right fist drove his head with a bang against the floor. Then he had hold of the gun again and pressed it against my side. I got hold of the barrel and pushed it down. There was a muffled report—a smell of powder—and I felt him stiffen and then go limp.

I twisted the gun from his hand and staggered to my feet. A wisp of white smoke was curling from the muzzle of the pistol. He lay still on the rug, and as I watched I saw a red stain on his shirt front. His coat had been open, and in the struggle his jacket had opened. He had no vest and the blood was pouring from his body and drenching his shirt.

I looked stupidly at the gun. I had heard nothing but a muffled thudding sound. There was a contraption on the muzzle of the gun. Though I had never seen one, I knew it was a silencer. I reckon it was the silencer which had saved my life, for it had caught in the lining of his coat pocket and given me a chance.

Feeling as though I would faint, I dropped into a chair, holding the weapon in my hand. The fellow looked dead, and I was too horrified to find out if his heart was beating.

Like most people, I'm not suspicious. So far as I knew I didn't have an enemy in the world. When the man came in

I thought he was another detective, but he was an assassin sent to murder me. Why? What for?

I laid the gun on the table beside my chair and wiped my reeking forehead. It was in the cards for me to be laying there dead or dying, instead of him. If his expression hadn't warned me, I wouldn't have been suspicious of the hand in his pocket. I would have supposed he was taking out a package or a letter that he wanted to show me—something bearing on the Ray case. On impulse I had let my foot drive, and that impulse had saved my life.

But now—how could I explain his presence here; his death, if he were dead? Who would believe my story? A doctor had to be summoned, and then I'd be arrested. God, what a situation!

I had to call the doctor. I phoned downstairs and asked them to send one in a hurry. Then I had an inspiration. I called Forman. I was shaking like a leaf during the few seconds it took to make the connection.

"Peter Hunter speaking," I said. "Forman, I've just shot a man. Can you get right over?"

"Yes, certainly. Give me the address."

I gave it to him.

"How come?" he demanded.

"Self-defense. He knocked at my door and I let him in. He pulled a gun and I jumped him. I shot him with his own gun."

"You ought to be in the Federal service," said Forman. "I can make it in ten minutes."

He hung up and I felt better. A minute later my bell rang and I admitted a Dr. Ross, who had an office in the building and with whom I had a bowing acquaintance. He wasted no words, but knelt beside the dead man and made a quick examination, tearing open the bloody shirt. In a few seconds he rose.

"Dead," he said. "Bullet entered the right side and plunged through into the heart. Bad business, Mr. Hunter. Did you shoot him?"

"Self-defense," I said with dry lips. "He pulled a gun on me. I struggled. He pulled the trigger but I depressed the muzzle. Otherwise I would be lying there."

"Fortunate for you," he said dryly. "I must report this, of course."

"There's the phone," I said.

"Who is he?"

"Don't know. Some gunman."

I WENT INTO my bedroom and closed the door while the doctor was telephoning. I had a sense of horrible injustice. Hadn't I gone through enough last night without having a thing like this happen? And I was bewildered as well as shocked. For no reason a man had come here to murder me—me, Peter Hunter, a good hardworking fellow who had never harmed anybody.

I pricked my ears as the apartment bell rang. The doctor opened the door and I looked out to see who it was. It was Forman. He took in the situation at a glance.

"Department of Justice operative," he said. "You're the doctor, of course. Dead?"

"Yes. I've just notified the police."

"Okay. I want to talk to Hunter." He saw me, came into the bedroom and closed the door.

"Buck up," he said with his heartening smile. "You're a

substantial citizen and I know a gunman when I see him. Tell me exactly what happened."

I told my story.

"You had a close shave," he commented. "Any notion why he wanted to kill you?"

"I tell you I never saw the man before. I've never had any trouble in my life."

"Haven't welched on gambling debts, I suppose?"

"I don't gamble."

"Own a gun?"

"No. I haven't fired one since I was a kid."

"Messing around with women?"

"Certainly not."

"Then," he said briskly, "let us assume that your visitation is connected in some way with the Ray case."

"But how can it be?"

He made an impatient gesture. "I'm a detective, not a clairvoyant. There must be an explanation for everything, and as there is no other reason for your being put out of the way, the Ray case must explain it. You found the body."

"But I've already identified it!"

"Hump. Maybe they want that identification to stand."

"What do you mean?"

He laughed. "I don't know, exactly. I'm baffled. The whole business doesn't make sense."

I was already getting my nerve back, and now I clapped my hands together.

"Forman, maybe you've hit on something," I said. "Listen. Tonight I got a fright—an awful shock. I thought I saw Ronnie Ray in a subway train."

"What's that," he cried sharply. "That's impossible!"

"I know it. It was some chance resemblance."

"Tell me about it!"

I told him of the incident of the subway platform at Seventy-second Street. He listened intently.

"As you say, a chance resemblance," he commented. "But, for the sake of argument, let us suppose that you made a mistake last night. That you did see Ray in that train. And Ray reported to some gang, or some accomplice, that you had spotted him. Wouldn't that account for the gunman?"

"It would not. Ronnie was my friend. I found him when he was earning nothing and made him famous. Why should Ronnie want me murdered?"

"I never met the man," replied Forman. "All accounts agree that he was a sweet, simple youth. Everybody agrees that he didn't appear to have a care in the world. Yet we know that the boy was being systematically robbed. For years he has been drawing out his money in cash and turning it over to somebody. That means that he was in continual fear of his life, or afraid of exposure for some crime."

"If he managed to appear carefree, he was a magnificent actor. It's obvious that this killer out there didn't call on you without a motive for his intended crime. It's quite possible that your recognition of the man in the subway train supplies the motive."

"Well, I don't believe it."

"I broke off because the doctor was admitting the police."

"Stay here," said Forman. "I'll talk to them."

A detective-sergeant came in, followed by two uniformed officers. I stepped to the bedroom door and looked into the living room. Forman showed his card to the sergeant, who introduced himself as Caffery of the homicide squad.

"Got the killer in there," he asked.

"Mr. Hunter shot this man with his own gun. Self-defense," said Forman.

The sergeant shrugged his shoulders. "When ain't it self-defense?" he sneered. "Let's have a look at this stiff." He walked over and looked down at the dead man and laughed.

"As I live and breathe!" he exclaimed "Louie the Loup!"

"You know him?" asked Forman.

"DO I KNOW him? He's been charged with three killings and got off. Probably got a chilled steel alibi for being here tonight! Well, Mr. Forman, just the fact that this is Louie the Loup makes it justifiable homicide. Come on out of that bedroom, you! Your name Hunter? Well, Hunter, you done a good job! In this man's town there ain't no use in trying protected gunmen. Thing to do is to plug them on sight. What did they have against you?"

"Nothing, so far as I know."

"They got plenty, and they'll probably try again. Shake, will you? Makes me feel good to see the Wolf lying there. *Loup* is French for Wolf, see? This guy is a Frog."

"Who's his principal?" asked Forman eagerly.

"He's been on his own lately. Used to work for Billy the Bronx Bum, but he's a handy man and they all use him. Don't you worry Mr. Hunter. You'll get a clean bill of health."

"Can't we get him out of my apartment?"

"Just as soon as the medico gets a look at him. Got to book you as a formality. The fresh air will do you good, the way you're probably feeling."

"I'll go along," said Forman. He took my arm and led me back into the bedroom.

"It's a break the sergeant knew the fellow," he said. "Otherwise the police would have given you a bad time. Lucky you caught me in. I went up to have another talk with the dumb woman who played the piano for Ray, and found she had moved without leaving an address."

"I forgot to tell you. She's vamoosed."

"Why? How do you know?"

I told him of my interview with Miss Lawton during the afternoon.

He laughed. "Don't blame the poor old girl for being annoyed," he said, "but we may need her in our business. If Ray was in the hands of criminals she must know something about it, and it looks as if she had been keeping quiet. Frightened herself, no doubt. I'll send out an alarm for her. She'll not get far."

I grinned. I didn't think she would, either.

Forman patted my shoulder. "You're vitally concerned in this business, my boy, and we'd better stick close. Mind if I move in with you?"

"Would you?" I asked eagerly.

"If your sight of Ray's double makes it desirable to wipe you off the face of the earth, you might get another call. I'll move in tonight. Let's be going."

The medical examiner was on the job and Caffery was anxious to get the formalities over with. At headquarters I made my statement, Forman got busy, and I was admitted immediately to bail.

In two hours I was back home, where only a slight stain on the rug gave evidence that a tragedy had occurred. In another half hour Forman arrived with his bags. We had a few drinks, discussed the business for an hour, and went to bed. And, though I had killed a man, I slept well.

10

LUNCH WITH BARBARA BOND

I HAD A session with Kittie Ketchum when I reached the office in the morning because the papers carried the story of the attempt upon my life and its result. I had to tell her everything, while she sat there with a pale face and frightened eyes.

"And you don't know why," she said finally.

"Unless he made a mistake."

"Pete," she said earnestly, "I know it has something to do with the Ray case. Maybe somebody heard you boasting at lunch yesterday."

"I wasn't boasting," I said angrily. "And I'm not frightened. If the police don't find this murderer, I will."

That was swank. To tell the truth, I'd had a fright and was willing to mind my own business; but Forman had moved in with me and seemed to assume that he could depend on me to help him. Also, he was certain that I was a focal point, starting from which the mystery could be solved.

"I've a boy soprano I want you to hear," she said shortly. "I've made an appointment at International to listen to him from a sound room at eleven."

"That's an idea," I admitted. "A boy soprano—maybe

that would please Madame Duplon. Who is he? Cost much?"

"He's been on a sustaining program for a month. It's a lovely voice, and suitable, I think, for a perfume program. We could build him up, maybe."

"Okay, I'll go up. Let's get our letters out," I said.

When we finished my phone rang and it was Barbara Bond.

"Peter," she said. "I've read the papers. I think you were marvelous. I want you to lunch with me at the Waldorf at twelve-thirty. Will you?"

"And why not?" I replied. When I hung up Kittie demanded to know what she said. "She thinks I'm marvelous," I said with a chuckle. Kittie snorted.

"She read about my heroic defense last night," I explained.

"Now you listen to me," Kittie commanded. "I love Barbara, but I know her. She's the richest girl in the States, and a beautiful blonde. Also she has no discretion, she's wild as a hawk, and she has no respect for her own neck. Don't you get any delusion that you can take Ronnie's place with her. She's going to use you. No doubt she has some crazy scheme that may cost you your life. For heaven's sake, Pete—"

"Aw, dry up, Kittie! She's just taking me to lunch."

"Will you promise not to do a thing she asks you without consulting me?"

"Who are you, my mother?"

Kittie grinned impishly. "Practically, if you want the truth. You haven't any more sense than a ten-year-old."

"Well, if it's anything I can discuss, I'll tell you about it."

"Atta boy," said my secretary, and went off with her note-book.

We heard the boy soprano. His top notes were too shrill and he sang without much expression. Kittie is a swell girl but not much of a musician. Neither am I, but I'm better than she is.

I sent her back to the office and at twelve-thirty I met Barbara in the Waldorf bar. She was in black like a widow and dazzlingly beautiful, though she didn't smile and there was a worried wrinkle between the eyes.

We sat down in a deserted corner of the bar. I ordered cocktails. She asked me about the night before, and I told her how everything happened.

"It's most amazing that you realized the situation," she said. "You're considerable of a man, Peter."

"Thanks. I was just lucky."

"Well, Thank God, you escaped. Now, Peter—are you absolutely, positively sure that it was Ronnie you—er—found, night before last."

"Of course. He had a letter of yours in his pocket."

"I know. The only note I ever wrote him," she said sadly.

"He had on Ronnie's clothes and—well I recognized him even though—"

I broke off. How could I tell her the face was nothing but a smear? She understood, though, because her pretty face twisted with pain.

"But there is a faint possibility you might be mistaken—"

I hesitated. I remembered the man on the subway train, and the deduction Forman made from it regarding the motive of the gunman.

"I—I don't think so."

She sipped her drink and was silent for a moment.

"I'm not supposed to say anything, but I must," she said. "Last night at midnight those people called me up."

"The fake kidnapers?"

She nodded. "They assured me that Ronnie is alive. They said—they said they had him with them night before last—in the group at the railroad."

"Barbara, you're not mad enough to believe them!" I protested.

"I have reason to believe them. They said they would let Ronnie sing a song to me—our song, 'Barbara Allen.' Pete, he did! He sang one verse, and it was he—there's no voice like it—"

"Barbara—"

"And then he said, 'Come soon,' she continued, almost weeping. Immediately the kidnaper said, 'Stay near the telephone. You'll get instructions.'"

"Barbara, it was an electrical transcription!"

"No, it wasn't!"

"Over a telephone wire you can't tell the original from the transcription—"

"I KNOW IT wasn't! Ronnie never sang 'Barbara Allen' over the radio. He didn't know the song. It's an old English ballad my nurse taught me. I sang it to him that last day. He said it was lovely and he promised to learn it and sing it over the radio especially for me."

"Then you never heard him sing it—"

"He took the music! It was in an album. He hummed it over with me. You know how she is, too shy to open his mouth in front of anybody. You know I had to agree that all the lights would be extinguished if he sang at my party!"

"I didn't know that, but I suppose he would stipulate it."

"So, that's why I know that Ronnie is alive and why I'm going to pay the ransom!" Barbara said. "I've been reproaching myself bitterly for losing my nerve and smashing through the railroad gates. I didn't sleep a wink."

"Barbara," I said earnestly, "please believe that Ronnie is dead. This is some trick."

"How can it be? Only Ronnie and I knew the significance of 'Barbara Allen.' How could these kidnapers know it if they haven't got him."

"Barbara, if they were on the level, they wouldn't have resorted to stopping you at the railroad crossing. They would have stopped their car when they reached the place where they had Ronnie, produced him, taken the ransom and let you both go. They planned to bring you up short, swarm over the car and take the money, perhaps carry you off for more ransom, because they had never had him in their possession. These fellows have no connection with Ronnie's disappearance. I know it. Ronnie is dead!"

"Then how do you account for his talking to me—"

"You said he sang—"

"He said, 'come soon,' in the most pathetic voice—"

"They faked his voice."

"Well, how do you account for 'Barbara Allen'?"

"I—I can't account for it," I admitted.

"I'm going to take the risk," she insisted, on the chance that you didn't find Ronnie but somebody dressed in his clothes."

"Tell me why they should dress somebody in his clothes and kill him."

"I don't know. I have the money ready, and, when the summons comes, I'll answer it."

From the set of her chin I knew it was useless to argue.

"Okay," I said. "You tell them you won't come a second time alone. Insist that you have a companion with you. I'll go with you. They'll consent. They want the money, don't they?"

"Peter, I wouldn't let you take the risk."

"I'll take any risk you do," I growled. "Let's go to lunch."

Barbara only picked at her food, and, frankly, I had no appetite. I was thinking of what I had let myself in for. I would have bet ten to one that Barbara and I would be murdered out of hand if we kept a rendezvous with these gangsters. And yet what kind of man would I have been if I hadn't volunteered?

When I returned to the office Kittie was excited.

"We've had a wire from an agent in Baltimore to listen in at two-thirty to a female baritone," she said. "He claims it's a perfectly angelic voice, quite different from Ronnie's, but equally thrilling. She's singing on a small station down there, but we can get it on the radio in your apartment."

"Female baritone," I said disgustedly. "I hate 'em."

"Nevertheless we'll go up and tune in," she said firmly. And so we did.

Forman was off about his business somewhere and Kittie and I had a high ball and tuned in on the Baltimore station. There was a jazz band on it, very bad, but it came through very well considering New York interference.

At two-thirty they announced Miss Iona Ivar, who would sing "Old Black Joe." I grinned derisively at Kittie, but the song began and in a second the singer had me.

Hers was a haunting, mellow voice, half way between contralto and baritone. She seemed splendidly trained, for her nuances were perfect and she could get emotion in a song like nobody's business. I tell you that the old chestnut brought tears to my eyes!

"Tune out," I said. "Wire this agent we'll be in Baltimore tonight and to have this woman on hand. Pack a bag and meet me at the station."

Kittie wiped her eyes. She'd been crying too. "They'll forget Ronnie Ray in a week," she said. What a find! What a find!"

11

MURDER

WE MET THE agent, whose name was O'Brien, at the Southern Hotel in Baltimore. He seemed nervous and there was a furtive look in his eye.

We shook hands and asked for the singer. "She's waiting in my suite," he said. "Ahem, after all, it may be years before television comes in."

Kittie looked at me and I looked at Kittie and we burst out laughing.

"Bad as that!" I remarked. "Probably this is one who ought to sing in the dark."

We didn't guess the half of it. Iona Ivars was a very fat, very big woman—and not the smiling, good-natured fat type. She had four chins and a surly, scowling moonface. She was shabby and she ought to have read soap ads, and taken the suggestion. Once a week, anyway. Her age, I suppose was about forty.

"Make her sing," I whispered.

She sang "Swanee River." Closing my eyes I was able to enjoy that song more than I ever had, and it has always been my favorite.

"Much obliged," I said when she had finished. "Mr. O'Brien, let's go into another room."

Kittie sighed. "Lovely voice, but impossible. Too bad."

"What are you talking about," I whispered. "Madame Duplon won't be jealous of this dame! How about her repertory, O'Brien?"

"Everything. Opera, French, German, Italian, and all the heart songs," Iona Ivar had been singing for nothing, and I signed a six months' contract with her at a hundred a week, with an option to renew at three times that amount for another six months. I knew that if I couldn't unload her on Perfumes of Arcady, small sponsors would grab her at that figure.

After that I talked with the woman like a Dutch uncle.

"You've got to dress decently and bathe frequently," I said. "This is your chance to get on the big time in a big way. The least you can do is what I tell you."

Tears were rolling down the big woman's cheeks. "I've been broke for a month," she said. "How do you suppose I can bathe when there isn't a bathroom in the dump where I live?"

I slipped her a century note on account, and then Kittie and I went to a motion picture show. For once Kittie agreed with me that I'd put over a deal.

"Of course she'll never be a popular idol like Ronnie," she said, "but that voice will make lots of money. Remember Kate Smith."

Kate Smith is pretty and a slender sapling compared to this behemoth, I told her, "but I'm betting she'll be making a thousand a broadcast soon."

Back in New York, Kittie and I had breakfast in the Penn Station, and separated. I took the subway uptown and at about half past eight, I let myself into my apart-

ment. I looked into the bedroom. Forman was in his twin
bed asleep. I took off my shoes so as not to wake him
and tiptoed into the bathroom, where I had a shower and
shaved. After that I went to the dresser and took out clean
linen. My elbow knocked the alarm clock off the dresser
top. It hit the floor and the alarm went off with a terrible
jangle.

"Excuse me, old man," I said, and glanced at Forman.
He didn't move.

I stared. There was something queer about the way he lay,
motionless on his back through that uproar. I rushed to the
bed, pulled down the blankets, which were up to his chin.
Inside they were covered with blood. So was his pajama
shirt. I touched him gingerly. His face was cold as ice.

I backed away, trembling. I rushed to the telephone.

"Get the police," I shouted to the operator. "Mr. Forman
has been murdered!"

And then I staggered to the divan and fell on it. This
time I fainted, went out cold. After all a man can stand
just so much. A pounding on the door awakened me—I
suppose only five minutes had gone by, but that's about as
long as a faint lasts. I let in the superintendent of the building and the cop on the beat.

"This is too much!" shouted the superintendent. "You've
got to move."

I laughed hysterically. Even the policeman laughed, but
stopped when he saw what was on the bed.

Things happened so fast in the next hour that I didn't
have time to think. Homicide men—medical examiner—
question on question. Finally it was over. The body was
carried away and I was left alone.

HERE I WAS out on bail on one homicide, and another following on its heels in my apartment. Fortunately, in this case, the killing had taken place shortly after midnight, according to the medical examiner, and I was boarding a train at Baltimore at that time with Kittie.

My absence was known and my return had been observed. And Sergeant Caffery, who, fortunately, had turned up on the case, knew that Forman was my friend and had moved in with me in case another attempt was to be made on my life. The police were convinced that whoever had sent Louie the Loup, had dispatched another assassin to accomplish what the first murderer had failed to do.

I was marked for death. And I was unaware of the identity of my enemy, and ignorant of his reason for wishing me put out of the way. A fine, honest, clever Department of Justice operative had given his life for mine. This time a knife had been used, which had been withdrawn from the heart of the detective and carried off by the murderer.

I couldn't stay in the place, so I packed a bag and moved to a hotel where I registered under an assumed name. I phoned the office that I wouldn't be in—fortunately Kittie hadn't arrived or she would have asked questions—and I went to bed, where I tossed for hours. I felt horribly about Forman. Curiously, I wasn't afraid for myself any more. I gritted my teeth and swore vengeance on the murderers. I'd get them—somehow. Along about noon I got up and went to the office. The business had to go on, and if I was fated to die in my prime, hiding out wouldn't save me.

Kittie followed me into the office and shut the door.

The extras were out, of course, and she knew what had happened.

"If we hadn't gone to Baltimore," she began, "you'd be dead, wouldn't you."

"Maybe not. With two men in the apartment it wouldn't have been so easy for the assassin."

"But the knife was meant for you," she persisted.

I shrugged my shoulders. "I suppose so."

She sat on the edge of my desk. "Peter," she said, "What do you know about this that I don't?"

"Nothing."

"You know something that menaces these people; otherwise they wouldn't try to kill you. What is it?"

"Kittie, I haven't an idea in the world who killed Ronnie Ray," I said earnestly. She screwed up her little face.

"Without being aware of it, you know something," she insisted. "Try to think. They're betrayed themselves to you in some way, and they are frightened of you. Something Ronnie may have told you which is the key to the whole mystery."

"Looking back," I said, "I can't remember that Ronnie ever told me anything of importance."

"Do you know what I've been doing all morning?" she asked. "I've been going over all checks paid by this office to Ronnie."

"What's the sense of that."

"Wait a minute!" she grinned at me, and came back with a stack of canceled checks.

"They total nearly seven hundred thousand dollars," she said. A hundred thousand the first year, five hundred thousand the second year, and nearly a hundred thousand so far this year.

"You got him incorporated last year so he doesn't have to pay his income tax until June first of this year, and it looks like the government and the state will have to whistle for their share of the inheritance tax unless that money is found. Now, all these checks were endorsed and deposited in the bank by him except two. She produced the two checks. One for a thousand, and one for fifteen hundred.

"These," she said, "were endorsed and apparently turned directly over to somebody. Here is his endorsement. Who is it?"

I looked at the endorsements. The signature on each was the same.

A.H. Warren.

"Who is A.H. Warren?" she demanded.

"Never heard of him."

"It occurred to me that this A.H. Warren might be the person to whom Ronnie Ray has been handing his money in cash."

"In which case A.H. Warren is the last person who would want Ronnie to stop broadcasting," I replied. "Just the same, it's worth investigating. Smart work, Kittie. Call up the bank, tell them who we are, and ask them for a line on Warren."

She left the room, but returned almost immediately, escorting a gigantic female at whom I had to take a second glance to recognize Iona Ivar.

Iona wore a new black outfit and a smart bonnet. Nothing in the world could make her attractive but she had done her best. There were spots of rouge on her moon-like countenance, lipstick upon her thick lips, and mascara beneath her big black eyes. She carried a large black book under her arm and placed it on a table. She smiled eagerly.

"Here I am," she declared. "I spent most of the money you gave me."

12

THE CLUE OF THE FAT GIRL

THE EVENTS OF the morning had driven from my mind the fact that I had told Iona Ivar to take a train for New York and report at my office, but here she was and I had to make the best of it.

"Please sit down, Miss Ivar," I said politely.

I heard the chair creak under her bulk and suppressed a smile.

"I hear you want me to take Ronnie Ray's place," she said.

"I don't know where you heard that," I said guardedly.

"Well, that's what O'Brien thought. I can sing the kind of songs Ray sang. You only heard me in plantation melodies, but—"

"I'm going to let the Duplons hear you sing," I told her, "but I doubt if they'll want you. I engaged you because I think you've got the stuff, and I can probably unload you on one of my clients."

"I'd like to work with Ray's accompanist," she said.

"She's a peculiar person. I doubt if she would work with you."

"You can't tell me anything about her," she said hotly.

"She may have gone high-hat, but she can't pull any of that on me."

"Then you know Miss Lawton?"

"Lawton! I knew her when she was Alice Warren," she retorted.

I stared at her stupefied.

"Alice Warren?" I asked after a second. "You mean her name is Alice Warren?"

"Sure. She played piano for me ten years ago in the Chautauqua circuit in the South."

"Is her middle initial H?" I demanded eagerly.

"I didn't know she had one."

"How do you know it's the same woman?"

"Because I wrote her a letter after recognizing her picture taken with Ronald Ray. I asked her if she didn't use to call herself Alice Warren, and she wrote back that she had changed her name because Lita Lawton was more euphonious. I wanted her to land me in radio, but she said she couldn't do anything for me.

"Oh, then, she admitted it?"

"Sure. What could she do? She didn't want me coming round and exposing this dumb gag of hers."

I almost jumped out of my chair.

"You mean Miss Lawton isn't dumb?"

"I never heard of anybody going dumb. Did you? When I knew her she could talk as well as anybody else."

I leaned back flabbergasted.

"Why do you suppose she should fake dumbness?"

The big woman laughed. "Just show business, like making Ronnie Ray sing in the dark. That's the bunk, of course."

I grinned at her. "You know, Miss Ivar, I think I'm going to like you."

She chuckled heavily. "I always said that a good-looker had only a fifteen minute start on a dame with brains. I've been batting around show business for twenty years, getting no breaks on account of my fat, but the boys used to be glad to come up to my room after the show was over and sit around having drinks and hearing me talk."

"You're not lying," I insisted. "You actually got a letter from Miss Lawton acknowledging her identity, and when you knew her she could talk?"

"I have the letter somewhere. Sure she could talk."

"I wrote her a check for a hundred dollars. "Go to a hotel and come back tomorrow afternoon. My secretary, Miss Ketchum, will make arrangements for an audition for the Duplons. That's all today."

She arose. "You're a good guy, Hunter," she said. "I was about at my last gasp when you turned up last night. I'll make good for you in a big way."

When she had gone, Kittie came in.

"A.H. Warren," she said, "is a woman, she closed her account at Chatham Bank a year ago."

"I can beat that," I said triumphantly. "A.H. Warren is Lita Lawton's real name."

Kittie flopped into a chair. "You don't mean it!"

"And the payments were probably salary payments, so they don't give us a line on the blackmailers. I shall now tell you something even more surprising. She isn't dumb. She can talk like anybody else."

"I don't believe it! Who told you?"

"Our fat find, Iona Ivar. It seems that Lawton played

accompaniments for her ten years ago. They exchanged letters a year ago, and Lawton admitted her identity."

"Imagine that old maid putting over a thing like that!" exclaimed Kittie. "What for? Of all the crazy—well, I never thought she was quite right."

"It was good showmanship, Kittie. Come to think of it, Ronnie's dumb accompanist helped a lot in the publicity the first few months."

"Yes, but how inconvenient!"

"Singing in the dark was inconvenient, too; and that had a lot to do with the ballyhoo that put him over."

Kittie nodded thoughtfully. "It's a cinch it wasn't Ronnie's idea. And I had her sized up as simple!"

"She's a fox," I agreed. "Tell the Duplons we have something for them to hear tomorrow afternoon. I'm going to make Ivar sing in the dark. If they see her before they hear her, all is lost."

"That's right. When they see her, Duplon won't want her and Madame Duplon will insist on having her. Peter, will you take care of yourself?"

"I'm applying for a permit to carry a gun."

"Yes, but—I'm terrified for you."

"Looks like I bear a charmed life."

"FAMOUS LAST WORDS," she retorted as she left the office. Her brash remark couldn't cover the fact that she was frightened for my safety. Kittie was a hundred per cent loyal, and we'd been together so long we were firm pals.

I began to jot down notes, as I always do when working out a problem.

The murder of Ronnie. Either revenge or the work of a crazy man, since killing him profited the murderer nothing.

The man in the subway train. Poor Forman thought that the attacks on me were to prevent me from broadcasting that I had seen Ronnie or his double. That theory meant that Ronnie was alive, but somebody wanted it believed that he was dead badly enough to have the person who had caught a glimpse of him murdered.

Well, I didn't believe that Ronnie was alive. Therefore the attempts to murder me had some other motive. Find the motive and I had the key to the mystery.

The people in communication with Barbara. They were criminal fakers, and the stage business they had arranged for her was bunk and nothing else. Eliminate them. Anyway that was my idea.

I couldn't think of anything else to jot down and my notes didn't clarify the situation. Muddled it. Looking back, I marvel at my own dumbness. The key to the mystery was right under my nose and I couldn't see it.

I was called down to Headquarters about that time and interviewed by the commissioner of police in person. The chief of the homicide squad was there and they questioned me for an hour. I kept nothing back. I told them about the glimpse I had had of a man who looked like Ronnie in the subway train, and repeated Forman's theory that it might really be he, which would account for the efforts to murder me.

"This cousin of Ray's has identified the body," said the commissioner, "but he's a stupid fellow. He hadn't ever been close to Ray, and naturally he wants him legally dead so that he can inherit what possessions he left and the vanished money, if it can be recovered. Miss Lawton, the accompanist, refused to go into New Jersey to look at the corpse and by the time we had authority to take her there she had disappeared. I don't understand how she could have escaped. He looked hard at the homicide chief. "It looks like very slovenly police work."

"I had two good men tailing her," the chief said. "They shadowed her to Mr. Hunter's office, and back to her hotel, When and how she got away they can't explain. But a dumb woman ought to be easy to pick up."

"It happens that she isn't dumb," I said, smiling.

It was like hitting them with a bombshell. I then explained what I had learned from Miss Ivar, after which I gave a lecture upon the publicity advantages of a dumb accompanist, and Ronnie's refusal to broadcast except in the dark.

"I never believed he was really afraid of the mike," I told them. "It was all showmanship, probably invented by Miss Lawton. Ronnie would never have thought of the stunts."

"And you believe that they were of assistance in making him famous?" I nodded. "They helped a lot in the beginning. You see, there is only just so much you can say about an artist's voice; but the papers will print columns upon personal idiosyncrasies."

"I see," said the commissioner. "Then, this Lawton woman's identification ought to be positive. So she must be found. The fellow apparently never had any dentistry done, he was never fingerprinted, and he had no distinguishing marks on his body. I don't blame the old girl for not wanting to look at his decomposed corpse.

"I understand that she received ten per cent of his earnings. That would be seventy thousand dollars. I'm informed she never filed an income tax statement. That gives us a grip

on her. Now, Mr. Hunter, holding you in connection with
the death of Louie the Loup is only a formality, and your
alibi in the Forman case cannot be controverted, particularly as we know that Mr. Forman moved in with you to
protect you in case of another attempt on your life. I'm
going to keep a man on guard in your apartment and I'll
have you shadowed wherever you go."

I hesitated. I didn't want to break faith with Barbara,
but I was positive that she was being victimized by those
in communication with her. Besides, if the police were
following me I couldn't accompany her as I had promised.

"Look here," I said, "I'm going to break a confidence,
but I think I'm justified." I then told the commissioner of
the attempt to make Barbara believe that Ronnie was alive
and could be ransomed.

HE LOOKED PUZZLED. "You saw a man who looked like
him in the subway. His voice sings a song which had special
significance for Miss Bond. Does that shatter your belief
that the man found dead at that wayside inn was Ray?"

"No," I said positively. "If Ronnie was in the hands of
kidnapers he wouldn't be riding in a New York subway
train. The song must have been an electrical transcription.
Turn one on a telephone wire and you can't tell it from the
original."

"But she said he didn't know the song, had never broadcast it—

"Ronnie wasn't as simple as he seemed or he couldn't
have carried on cheerfully when all his earnings were being
taken away from him," I argued. "Maybe he did know the
song. Maybe he had made a private transcription—

"Miss Lawton, of course, would know if he had. Another reason for finding her."

"That's right. I hadn't thought of that."

"Trying to cash in on another gang's snatches is an old game," said the commissioner thoughtfully. "Mr. Hunter, they're going to take the girl's two hundred thousand in cash, and in all probability, grab her and hold her for ransom. They'll probably shoot you out of hand. Are you game to accompany her?"

"I told her I would," I said stoutly. "I've got to go through."

"Very good. We'll have her residence covered. We'll have a car waiting to follow you and her, assuming that they consent to your accompanying her. We'll have a code ready to instruct all police cars as soon as you start. There is a good chance we can round up these scoundrels without endangering your lives, but you understand there's a big risk."

"If Barbara finds out—

"We know that Ronald Ray is dead. Therefore police surveillance isn't going to harm a captive they haven't got," the commissioner pointed out.

"Okay, I agree," I nodded.

He offered me his hand and we shook. I shook hands with the homicide chief. "You'll be trailed from now on, said the chief. "And I hope you won't mind a cop in your quarters."

"I'd love him," I said with a grin.

13

WILD RIDE

THAT NIGHT I had dinner with Kittie. I told her the arrangements for my safety, which pleased her. I didn't tell her about my arrangement with Barbara, because she would have made a fuss about it. It seemed that she had lunched with Barbara that day, and Miss Bond hadn't told her anything.

After dinner we went to a picture show. I took her home and then went to my apartment. I found a plain-clothes-man drinking my Scotch and making himself at home. His name was MacCarthy. He was a smart looking young fellow who told me his orders were not to close an eye. It seems my lodgers were to be on eight hour shifts.

I was tired and I started to undress. Just then the phone rang and the cop answered it. "For you, Mr. Hunter," he told me. "Some doll."

Kittie, of course. I picked up the receiver. It was Barbara.

"I'll be waiting at the entrance to your apartment house in ten minutes," she told me. "Then you got the call," I said excitedly.

"Yes. They agreed that you could accompany me."

"Where do we go?"

"I can't tell you that," she replied and hung up. I turned to the cop. "How do I get Captain Mullins?"

"He'll be at home. Bryant 4-7652."

I called Mullins and he answered immediately.

"Hunter speaking," I said, "starting out in ten minutes with Miss Bond."

"She'll be followed from her house. We'll be close to you all the time. I'm going out on the job myself. The state police are waiting for the warning. Look out for yourself."

"Can I get a gun somewhere?"

"Let me talk to the officer on duty. I'll tell him to give you his."

He spoke to the officer who reluctantly turned over a heavy police revolver, and some extra cartridges.

"I'm not crazy to be left alone in this dump," he grumbled.

"You can have the night off after I leave," I said. "And maybe you won't be needed around here any more."

"Why?"

"I may not come back." I shuddered after I spoke. Why not? I'm no hero. After what I'd already been through I should have been in the hospital with nervous prostration, and here I was going out with a crazy woman to meet a mob of gunmen, whether Barbara and I would be a couple of corpses before the police caught up with us depended on how they felt.

I began to think it was suspicious that they let me accompany her. I wished she'd get a blow-out on the way up. With trembling fingers I was fastening my collar and tie. I thrust the gun into the side pocket of my top coat. It was too big to go in my hip pocket. A lot of use it would be to me! More likely to shoot myself than anybody else.

I glanced at the clock. The ten minutes were up. For no reason I shook hands in the lingering fashion with the cop, and then went down the corridor to the elevator like a man going to his own execution.

Barbara was parked outside the entrance where no parking was allowed, and the doorman was arguing with her. A glance at her gave me nerve. She was smiling gaily, and as usual looked like a million dollars. She was in black with a little black three-cornered hat. I climbed in beside her and we were off.

Maybe you know what Broadway traffic is in the Seventies? It was my first experience with what some call an expert driver and some call a nut. We tore up Broadway. When we came to a red light we turned right into a side street. If the red light was on at Columbus she made a left turn regardless, and headed back onto Broadway through the next block. Occasionally she slowed to forty.

"You're going to get pinched," I warned. How I hoped she would be!

She seemed to know on what corners cops were stationed and where they weren't, and she ran through signals with impunity at the latter spots. Once a red light caught us square and there was a car stopped ahead near the curb to prevent one of her famous right turns. Did it? Barbara just ran up on the sidewalk and around the corner that way, narrowly missing a colored man coming down the side street who plunged into a doorway with a howl of mortal terror.

At Ninety-sixth street she caught the signals right and

went tearing down into Riverside Drive. She was going sixty on the Drive. I glanced at her and her chin was thrust out and her eyes were dancing with excitement. A fat chance police cars would have to keep up with this girl. Did she think she was driving an airplane? Signals red. Back into West End Avenue. Houses and pedestrians were just a blur.

"Where are we going?" I ventured.

"George Washington Bridge."

"You'll get there ahead of time," I said mournfully.

"We're followed, of course. I've got to lose them."

My hand went into my right coat pocket and the touch of the revolver butt gave me courage. A drink would help, but it hadn't occurred to me to bring a bottle.

IN FIVE MINUTES, so it seemed, we were going up the incline to the big bridge. There are speed regulations on the bridge, and she ignored them. I hoped they would pinch us at the other side, but she braked and we went through slowly, paid the toll and went respectably through the approaches until we swung into the Hudson River Boulevard.

Once in the country Barbara proceeded to show me what the new cars could do. I watched the speedometer needle hit seventy—eighty—eighty-five—eighty-eight—.

"For God's sake!" I pleaded.

"Silly, there's no danger! I always drive fast—"

"A blow-out—"

"I always have new tires."

A motorcycle siren blew as we whizzed past a state cop. Instead of slowing up she stepped on the gas. I closed my eyes so as not to see the speedometer. I looked back. That cop's headlight was back there and getting less bright at every second. She was dropping him with ease.

I began to hate Barbara Bond. She wasn't human. She was a Valkyrie riding the wind. And if she could lose a motorcycle cop, what chance did Captain Mullins and his outfit in the following car have to get near enough to be useful?

By and by the motorcycle headlight behind disappeared. Either the cop had quit or we had gained miles on him. I stole a look at the speedometer. Ninety-two miles an hour. Motor car manufacturers ought to be put in jail for making cars that will go so fast. Maybe fifteen minutes went by while we burned up the road. Suddenly she slowed, and a moment later swung left into a side road. I took a despairing look into the mirror. No headlights visible behind. And they'd never find us!

Barbara was creeping—for her—at about fifty miles an hour.

"Where are we?" I asked bitterly.

"Bear Mountain Reservation. Three red flashes are the signal, and this time I'm going to stop."

I didn't say anything, but stealthily drew from my pocket the police revolver. I cocked it. Anyway my hair had already turned white. We were on a winding road going up an incline. Bear Mountain is a big park up near West Point, and in the spring of the year it is not much frequented.

An ideal place for a murder. Our murder.

My toes occasionally touched a black bag on the floor. I knew what was in it. Two hundred thousand dollars in cash—to ransom a man I knew had been dead for weeks. Well, Barbara could afford to lose two hundred grand. She was rich. It was our lives I was thinking about. Where were the state police who had been warned? Where was Mullins, the four-flushing chief of the homicide squad?

"The signal!" said Barbara between clenched teeth. Up ahead at the top of the hill a red eye appeared, disappeared, shone again, and for a third time. We were slowing down.

"Peter, you're a peach!" said Barbara. "We'll soon know, eh?"

"Too soon," I muttered.

She had slowed to twenty miles an hour. We were gliding up the hill when Barbara suddenly gave a gasp and jammed on the breaks.

I stared. I suppose I turned green and my hair stood on end. For standing in the road in the full glare of the headlights, waving his right arm in friendly greeting was—*Ronald Ray*. There he stood, bareheaded, clad in his usual costume of brown tweed jacket and blue trousers.

"Oh, Ronnie, Ronnie!" cried Barbara hysterically.

Ronnie stepped out of the road and out of the range of the headlights, but two men appeared, one on each side of the car. The door on my side swung open.

"Get out," commanded this fellow.

"Get out, Miss Bond," said the man on the other side. "Hey, Ronnie come here!"

"Where's the money?" demanded the fellow who had ordered me out.

I picked up the bag in my left hand as I stepped into the road.

"Ronnie, darling!" screamed Barbara shrilly. "Oh, Ronnie!"

"Here's your swag," I said to my man. He took my bag in his left hand and suddenly pulled a revolver.

14

LOST FRIENDS

I HAD THRUST my gun back in my pocket as the kidnaper appeared, but my right hand was still grasping the butt.

"Got you!" said this hood through clenched teeth. My weapon was cocked. It was out, and I fired point-blank at him. The bullet tore out of my gun a fraction of a second before his went off. His bullet whizzed past my left ear. He was only two feet away and my slug hit him square in the chest.

A weapon blazed from the thicket a dozen feet away and I plunged into the thick woods at the right. There was no question the brute had intended to shoot me after relieving me of the ransom money. I had never fired a revolver without sighting along the barrel, but one couldn't miss from my distance.

Now they would shoot me down like a dog. I went plunging through the woods, stepping on branches that crackled as loud as gun shots, or so it seemed to me. Shots were being fired at me, at least a dozen. I bumped into trees, tripped over a tree root, fell, sprang to my feet, and ran on wildly in the pitch black night.

And suddenly I heard a starter snarl and then a motor car in first speed and then the roar of a car traveling fast

in high. I dropped flat, but there were no more shots, no
pursuit. I lay there for five or six minutes, but everything
was quiet. I concluded that they had piled into Barbara's
car and made their escape with her two hundred thousand
dollars.

Had they killed Barbara or carried her off? I had to
find out. I got to my feet and began to work my way back
toward the highroad. It was an unlighted road and I was in
a dense woods, and it took me at least ten minutes before
I blundered back to the macadam.

I didn't know how near I was to the spot where the car
had stopped. I didn't know where I was, except that I had
pavement under my feet instead of dried leaves. I peered
through the darkness and saw nothing, but in a couple of
minutes I heard the unmistakable sound of motorcycles
driven at high speed.

In a moment I saw two headlights coming up the grade.
State police. I stepped into the middle of the road and held
up my arms. In a second or two the headlights lighted me.
Immediately I dropped my arms and ran for the ditch.
And in another second two state policemen jumped off
their machines.

"Come out!" one of them called. "We've got you covered!"

If I had been a criminal I could have picked them both
off, for they were in the light and I was in the shadow. But
I stepped forth with my arms above my head.

"Who are you?" demanded one officer, while the other
stepped up behind me and patted my coat. He found my
gun and took it away.

"Name of Peter Hunter."

"You're the companion of Miss Bond. Where is she?"

"Carried off by the kidnapers, I guess," I said. "You guys are late, as usual."

One of the cops turned a flashlight in my face.

"It's Hunter. Snow-white hair," he said.

"You let them kidnap her, did you?" said the second cop. "You're a hell of a guy!"

"I shot one of them, I think. You ought to find the body somewhere along here."

"Get on your bike, Bill, and look for it," he said. "I'll hold this guy."

Bill had been gone five minutes when a big motor car came roaring up the hill. My captor made flashlight signals and it came to a stop a few yards below us. Police poured out of the car, headed by Captain Mullins.

"What's happened? Who have you got?" he demanded. "Oh, Hunter!"

"He let the kidnapers get away, and they seem to have carried Miss Bond off with them," said the cop.

"So you muffed it," said Mullins scornfully.

"I muffed it! Where in hell were you?" I said angrily. "You were supposed to be right on top of us."

"How the devil could we keep up with that wild woman?" he retorted. "The old bus won't travel more than seventy-five."

We were interrupted by the return of the second motor cop.

"I've been a mile up the road," he said. "No bodies laying round. This guy is talking through his hat."

"They picked up the man I hit and carried him off in Barbara's car. You're wasting your time. Go after them."

"Where does this road go?" demanded Mullins.

"Winds round and hits the Hudson Boulevard above five miles up," explained the cop.

"Well, it's watched from here to the Catskills. Her car is known," said Mullins. "You motorcycle men better go after them, though."

"This fellow, okay?"

"I'll answer for him."

THE CAPTAIN TOOK me by the arm and led me to the police car.

"Get in," he said, "We'll drive down to the highroad and await developments."

"You've a new kidnaping case to worry about," I said bitterly. "They'll ask plenty for Barbara, and they already have her two hundred grand."

He and I sat in the back seat. There were two cops in front, and a couple standing on the running board.

"We're out of our jurisdiction," said the captain, "but we're working with the State so that's all right. Suppose you tell me exactly what happened.

"They made good," I said. "They produced Ronnie Ray."

"What?"

I nodded. "Used him as a decoy. He stepped into the range of our headlights and waved to Barbara. She had already got their signal and was going slow. When she saw him, she jammed on the brakes and they had us."

"You mean Ronnie Ray. But he's dead!"

"Well, he certainly looked like Ronnie Ray," I said." I thought I saw a ghost."

"Skip it. What else happened?" Mullins asked. I told him the rest.

"You used your head," he said. "They were going to kill you."

"That's what I thought. Another one of them was shooting at me when I dove into the woods."

"This will be the fellow you saw in the subway train," said Captain Mullins.

"Maybe. If I hadn't seen Ray's dead body I'd certainly think it was Ronnie. Of course he was in cahoots with the criminals."

"Or he did what they told him because he was covered with a gun."

"Well, Miss Bond recognized him. She went all to pieces."

"That proves it was Ray," said Mullins slowly.

"I don't know," I answered, "she was engaged to Ronnie, but she had only met him two or three times. She doesn't know him as well as I do."

"But you'd say it was Ray?"

I nodded. "He or his ghost."

"You identified the body on general impression, but the face was unrecognizable," said the police captain. "This fellow has Ray's face."

"That's right," I agreed.

While we talked the car had turned and was moving swiftly back toward the river road. When we hit it the fellow at the right of the driver signaled with a flashlight, and from four places ahead flashes answered.

"When she turned up the river," said Mullins, "we radioed the news all along the line. We had the road perfectly covered only—he laughed with embarrassment—" somehow we never thought of the Bear Mountain Reservation.

They can't come back on this road without being nabbed. Every car on this road will be stopped and searched."

"You'll find Barbara's car abandoned on the Reservation," I told him. "You're up against clever people, Captain."

Our car moved up river. Every half mile or so a motorcycle cop showed, and on side roads police cars were stationed. It didn't look as if a gnat could slip through the cordon, but, at five in the morning, we learned that the criminals had slipped through somehow.

Mullins and I hadn't spoken for a long time. I was dead with fatigue and excitement and despair. Barbara's captors were ruthless. God knew what treatment she would receive at their hands.

15

THE BOY DETECTIVE

AT ELEVEN I woke up. The policeman in the living room was talking to somebody. "You'll have to wake him," this somebody was saying in a high-pitched voice. "I have no time to waste."

I rolled out of bed and opened the bedroom door.

"Do your duty," I commanded. "Throw him out, whoever he is."

"I am Wooster Williams, special agent of the Department of Justice," said the high-pitched voice. I looked at him through eyes heavy with sleep.

"Cock-a-doodle-doo," I jeered. "Park yourself, mister. When I've had my bath and dressed, I'll give you a few minutes of my time if I happen to feel like it."

The Federal man smiled confidently. "You'll feel like it," he said.

I closed the door and went into the bathroom, grinning. The Department of Justice must be running out of operatives, I thought, if they hired this hobbledehoy out there. He was a thin, blond youth with small, nondescript features. He gave an impression of utter insignificance. At a glimpse I would have put him down as under twenty. I found out later that he was thirty, and not a person to be sneezed at. Anyway, I took my time and kept him waiting twenty minutes. When I emerged, he was sitting in the living room at a window with his nose deep in a volume of my limited edition of Casanova.

"That will contaminate you, young fellow," I said with a grin. "Put it down."

"You've been bunked," he retorted. "A bad translation, and much abridged."

As I hadn't had time to read any of it myself I had no answer to that.

"Suppose we go in your bedroom. You can send down for breakfast," he suggested.

As I said, his voice was high-pitched. No doubt he sang tenor, but I'd had a look at a pair of cool gray eyes and decided to stop kidding him. He followed me into the bedroom and sat on my disordered bed while I phoned down for ham, eggs and coffee.

"I am familiar with your adventure of last night. I know everything you told Captain Mullins," he said. "I've studied Forman's notes and know his theories. We are picked men in our department, Mr. Hunter. We have an *esprit de corps* like no other organization. When we lose a man we punish his killer. We don't bother with red tape—"

"I know. You say 'Hello, John,' and pull the trigger," I replied. "I read about Dillinger. You're sort of young for a job like that, Mr. Wooster."

"Wooster Williams. I am thirty years old. I was sheriff of Butte, Montana at twenty-seven. I took Handsome Hanson and his two pals single-handed."

My mouth opened. "You mean to say you're that guy?"

"I'm not boasting," he said with a pleasant smile. "I have

an unfortunate appearance, and I have to establish confidence."

"Okay. Now what can I do for you?"

"On two occasions you've seen the ghost of Ronald Ray?"

"No ghost. Flesh and blood."

He drew forth the longest and fattest cigar I ever saw and lighted it. He looked like a baby in mischief as he emitted a cloud of pungent smoke.

"Now, either the electrocuted man in New Jersey was not Ronald Ray, or this is his double."

"I sort of deduced that myself," I said sarcastically.

"In the subway you were so sure it was Ray that you tried to board the car in which he was riding?"

"Right," I said.

"Last night when he stepped into the glare of the headlights, you not only recognized him, but Miss Bond, his fiancée, was also convinced that she was looking at her lover?"

"Right again."

"Then let us assume that this person was Ronald Ray."

"Assume what you like," I said curtly. "I know he's dead."

"We know that Ray was being bled of all his earnings. That means that somebody had a hold over him—blackmailers who could send him to prison or the chair for some crime. For their own reasons they kidnaped him—

"Thereby losing five thousand dollars a week," I pointed out.

"The game couldn't continue. They figured upon getting a big ransom from Miss Bond, perhaps collecting two or three ransoms. They used him as a decoy—you saw them do it. In a few weeks they expected to get half a million or

a million. Why wait a year or two collecting it in install-
ments from his radio earnings?"

"Look here—"

"There was a slip-up the first time. Miss Bond lost her
nerve—"

"She was rightly suspicious," I objected. "She has no
nerves."

"He sang to her a song significant only to her—"

"An electrical transcription," I insisted.

"He hadn't made one—"

"Listen, Wooster Williams," I said testily. "You may be
quick on the trigger, but your theory is full of holes."

"Now they have both Miss Bond and Ray in their
hands—"

"If you know everything, why bother calling on me?" I
yelled.

HE CHUCKLED LIKE a kid. "I don't know a damn thing,"
he said in quite a different manner. "You're the guy who
has swallowed the key to the mystery. I want you to cough
it up."

"Okay! If I swallowed this key it must have been inside
a capsule. I don't know it. Now, you listen to this. Somebody who hated Ray killed him in a horrible manner after
decoying him up to that roadside inn. Another gang found
his double, and have cashed in on it. My theory is as good
as yours."

"All right. Who had reason to hate him?"

"Almost every woman's husband or boy-friend."

"Rot! What have these criminals got against you?"

"Nothing whatever," I admitted.

"On the contrary, you know who they are—"

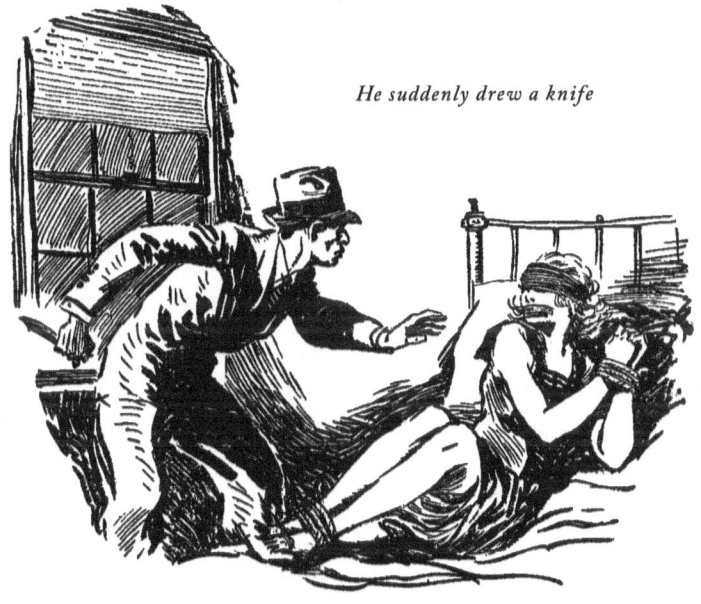

He suddenly drew a knife

"Say, if you're insinuating—"

"Don't get sore," Williams said. "What I mean is that you can blow them sky high if you remember something. I'd like to see what a hypnotist could do with you."

"Well, Mr. Department of Justice, you just try that on. Come to think of it, my secretary, Miss Ketchum, told me almost the same thing yesterday."

He grinned widely. "There you are! Am I a sap or am I a sap?"

"You and Kittie are both saps. I don't know a thing."

He rose. "I'm going down to have a talk with this secretary of yours. She sound interesting."

"Well," I said. "You're excused. Here comes my breakfast. Tell her I'll be down in an hour."

"Think," he commanded from the door. "Go over everything connected with your association with Ray. Over and over. When you least expect it, you'll hit on it."

"When you get through work at night," I jeered, "you probably put in the evening with an astrologer."

But Wooster Williams wasn't listening. The outer door slammed on my last word.

"Brash cub," I muttered and attacked my ham and eggs. "Hypnotist, eh? Poor old Forman was worth ten of him."

Just the same, people don't exert themselves to kill a person unless they have a reason, and both Kittie and the new Federal dick thought that my elimination was on the cards because I was a menace to the unknown criminals. Forman had suggested that the first attempt on my life was because I had seen Ronald Ray's double in the subway train—that somebody didn't want me to withdraw my identification of the body in the Jersey inn.

As this double of Ronnie's was in the hands of persons who wished Barbara Bond to believe that her fiancé was alive, this didn't seem a good reason. It looked to me as though I had been allowed to accompany her so that I could be murdered handily when they captured her. So it was probable that the kidnapers were the people who had sent Louie the Loup after me; and, when he failed, dispatched a second assassin who had killed poor Forman by mistake. But their reason was not to prevent me from broadcasting that Ronnie was alive.

I tried to recall all the talks I had had with Ronnie during our business association. Something he had told me might be the key that Kittie and Wooster Williams spoke of.

But I'd had singularly few intimate talks with Ronnie. He was a fellow who gave the impression of being candid, but who had nothing much to tell; not much on the ball, in fact. I'd learned more about him from the newspaper obituaries than I'd ever learned from his lips. Getting interesting material out of him for publicity purposes had been very difficult. The stuff he told was prosy and humdrum. He'd never been much of anywhere, and nothing of any consequence had ever happened to him. I'd faked a lot of stuff in order to get space in the papers for him.

Wooster Williams

I was riding downtown on the train when I had a flash. Maybe I'd been barking up the wrong tree. Maybe it wasn't Ronnie's revelations I ought to be trying to remember, but Lila Lawton's. That woman was weird, mysterious. She was the brains behind Ronnie Ray. And I knew, now, that she was a faker. Pretending to be dumb for years, inventing the hocus-pocus of singing in the dark... And disappearing off the map... She'd disappeared because she knew more than she wanted to tell. Undoubtedly she must know who the people were who were bleeding Ronnie of his earnings.

Now what had she ever said to me that might endanger the liberty of these criminals and murderers? Nothing. She had never spoken. We had communicated by means of slips of paper, and these were strictly business matters. Except the day she came to tell me she was going away.

Just the same, the thing to do was to find her; make her talk, use that tongue of hers. Well, the commissioner of

police had the same idea and had the whole force searching for her.

I got off at my station and went to the office. Kittie and
Wooster Williams were sitting at my desk, their heads
close together, laughing, chatting, apparently on friendly
terms.

I didn't like that.

16

THE LAST STRAW

"ANYTHING PARTICULAR, MR. Hunter?" asked Kittie demurely. "I was just going to lunch with Mr. Williams."

"Go ahead," I said shortly.

"Any news of Barbara?" she said.

"Ask him. He knows everything."

"Miss Ketchum naturally thought her captors might have communicated with you," said Williams, with his grin.

"They haven't."

Kittie laid a hand on my arm as I occupied the chair she vacated.

"You shouldn't have allowed her to go."

"Try stopping that girl from doing what she wants."

"You certainly shouldn't have gone with her."

"I'm glad I went," I said defiantly. "Have a nice lunch."

"Okay, if you feel like that!"

"Don't forget to concentrate," said Williams from the door.

I didn't answer him, but began to inspect the papers Kittie had laid on my desk. Looking back on it, I was leading a weird life at that time. Plugging away in the office in the daytime, buried in the routine of an advertising business, and running round the country at night shooting and being shot at.

And I was frightfully worried about Barbara. I hadn't played a heroic part. I hadn't done anything for her. But it had all begun and ended in a minute; the sight of Ronnie's ghost, which has unnerved me; the fellow who had tried to shoot me; the other one firing from the bushes. If I hadn't plunged into the woods I'd have been a corpse in another second. And Barbara was a fine, brave, generous girl; beautiful, high spirited—God, if they had killed her! No, they would consider her valuable. What they wanted was ransom. She would be safe. She had to be.

About two thirty Kittie came back. We talked everything over, and I took another wigging for risking my life.

"Mr. Williams says that you're to be more carefully guarded," she said. "He's certain that, through you, this whole business will be cleared up; and he's seeing to it that you take no more risks."

"I'm not going to have that squirt under foot," I said savagely. "Have you got a crush on him?"

"Sure," she said pertly. "So what?"

"So nothing. How about the audition for Iona Ivar?"

"The Duplons will hear her tomorrow at two. What hotel did she go to?"

"Eh? I don't know. You don't have to worry about her. She'll be in this afternoon."

Kittie nodded. "It's an appointment she won't miss, poor soul. Mrs. Duplon is half sold on her because she's cheap, and I told her she had a wonderful voice, but wasn't at all good looking."

"It's a better break than Duplon deserves. Though she'll never help the perfume business like Ronnie did."

"Well," said Kittie. "It's not beyond the bounds of possibilities that we'll get Ronnie back. Mr. Williams thinks so."

"You didn't see the body. I did. Ronnie is dead."

"Well, I hope not."

"How about dining with me tonight?" I asked in a different tone.

"Oh, I'm sorry. I didn't think you'd ask me. I—er— agreed to dine with Mr. Williams and discuss the case. He's sure the solution is in this office."

"He's sure of everything," I said grumpily. "Well, enjoy yourself."

"He's really very amusing."

"Sophomore," I sneered.

Kittie laughed. "Well, I never got through high school, myself."

Along about four o'clock I had shaken off my troubles and was actually accomplishing some business when Kittie ushered Sergeant Caffery into the office. The sight of him brought everything back.

"Sorry to interrupt you, Mr. Hunter," he said. "I see you're on the front page again today."

"That kind of publicity doesn't do my business any good. Have a chair, Sergeant. Have I got to go down to headquarters again?"

"Well, now," he said. "I come about something else."

"Yes? What?"

"You know a woman name Iona Ivar?"

I laughed. "Don't tell me she's been getting drunk and disorderly?"

"No," he said slowly. "Not exactly. Were you going to put her on the perfume hour in place of Ronnie Ray?"

I gaped at him. "Now how on earth—say, are the police butting into the advertising business?"

"We got troubles of our own, Mr. Hunter. Plenty. Was she going to work for Perfumes of Arcady?"

"I heard her in Baltimore a couple of nights ago and put her under contract, since you're interested," I explained. "I was going to let her try out for Mr. Duplon, but I don't know whether he would engage her. Would you like to see the report of this office for the fiscal year?"

"WOULDN'T UNDERSTAND IT," replied the sergeant. "The reason I mentioned it is because she ain't going to sing on any radio. She's dead. Say, for God's sake don't faint!"

"I won't," I said faintly. "She was very fat. Heart attack?"

"Kind of. A knife in the heart."

"M-m-murdered!"

He nodded. "Found her a couple of hours ago. Knifed in the small hours of the morning, according to the doctor."

I wiped my forehead. I had to hold onto myself or I would have fainted.

"A bread knife," he said. "Plain wooden handle. And tied by a string to the handle was a card. Have a look at it."

He handed me a piece of pasteboard such as one finds at hotel desks and upon which one scribbles a name and address. Printed neatly on the card were these words:

Iona Ivar unit never take the place of Ronald Ray.

I laid it down. I blinked my eyes, which were full of tears. The poor creature! Her first break. Comfort and ease and fame, perhaps; and, suddenly, death. And in a sense it was my fault. I'd brought her to New York.

But I hadn't told anybody except Kittie that I planned to put her on the perfume hour. Of course the poor woman had taken too much for granted. Probably she had boasted she would succeed Ronald Ray. Most likely she had lots of acquaintances in New York, fellow singers, actors. The rumor had got out through her. And now she was dead.

"Queer, ain't it?" remarked the sergeant. "Tell me what you know about her."

"Wire John O'Brien, her agent in Baltimore. I don't know anything about her," I answered. "She was in here yesterday and I told her to report back this afternoon. I was expecting her now."

"Ray is dead," said the sergeant. "Who would want to prevent her from getting the job? Somebody is going to get it."

I shook my head. "I'm about at the end of my rope, Sergeant. This finishes me. Any minute I'll be a candidate for Bellevue."

"We found a contract with your office in her handbag," he said. "And this card is how I knew she was going to sing on Ray's hour."

"I know, I know," I muttered.

"How about relatives?"

"I know nothing about her, but this office will pay the funeral expenses. It's the least we can do."

The sergeant rose. "That's pretty decent, too. Watch your step, Hunter. You ain't out of the woods."

"I'm getting so I don't care what happens to me."

He patted my shoulder like the good fellow he was, and

went heavily on his way. I stretched my arms out on my desk and laid my head on them and wept like a baby.

Somehow I felt even worse about this poor woman than I had about Ronnie Ray or Forman. And when Kittie came in and found me she broke down and wept with me. The sergeant had told her what had happened on his way out.

"I'm breaking my date with Wooster Williams," she said finally. "You mustn't be alone this evening."

I squeezed her hand. "You're a good kid, Kittie," I said.

17

THE ELECTRICAL TRANSCRIPTION

THE POLICE FOUND Barbara's car late that afternoon, abandoned in a field off a dirt sideroad across the state line in Pennsylvania. There was dried blood on the carpet in the tonneau, which meant that they had carried off the man I had wounded or killed along with Barbara.

There was a lot of newspaper excitement for days after that. Police of the city and state ran in circles. The papers hounded me. The headlines screamed:

RONNIE RAY ALIVE

The spectacular murder of Iona Ivar and its connection with the Ray case was played up in a sickening fashion. No demand, however, came from the kidnapers of Barbara. Barbara had been an orphan for ten years and had no near relatives. Her vast fortune was controlled by a bank and her trustees, who had no authority over her enormous income but sat on the principal like a lot of bulldogs.

The authorities had notified the bank that it would be prosecuted if it paid a ransom to Barbara's kidnapers, while her disappearance was good reason to refuse payment on any checks drawn by her which might be presented. The

kidnapers had the richest girl in New York and their prospects of cashing in on her were slight.

Kittie accused me of being in love with Barbara. Well, I
was fascinated by her plenty. I couldn't sleep nights thinking of the horrible fate in store for her if they couldn't
squeeze money out of her. She had played fair with them—
the money in the little black bag was not marked, and it
was all in hundred dollar bills, as they had demanded. The
chance of tracing it was slight.

Of course the authorities were working hard on the Iona
Ivar case. The employees of the little hotel in which she
had been killed were grilled until they were toasted brown.
I suppose everything was done that could be done—and
nothing was being accomplished so far as I knew.

If it hadn't been for Kittie, my business would have gone
completely to pot. I had a perfectly magnificent state of
jitters. Three days dragged by with a policeman always on
guard in my apartment, another sitting unobtrusively in
the anteroom of the Hunter Agency. Wooster Williams
was buzzing round me like a mosquito. He and Kittie
were going over our records, studying everything that had
a bearing on Ronnie Ray. Every day I had a session with
the police commissioner or Captain Mullins, and we went
over and over the whole thing.

In the mail which the postman delivered at noon on the
third day after the tragedy at Bear Mountain was a package
about twelve or thirteen inches square and an inch thick.

This package was addressed to Lita Lawton, care the
Hunter Agency. It was the only piece of mail which had
come for her. While she had authorized me to open and
read any communications which might come for her, I

didn't feel like doing it; and I had Kittie call up police headquarters and tell them that we had the package.

"Captain Mullins says he's coming up personally to open
it," she reported. "Wonder what's in it."

She lifted it. "Light," she commented. "Advertising
matter, most likely. Oh, Pete, why don't we hear from
Barbara?"

"For heaven's sake don't bring that up! I'm near crazy
now."

"You're hard hit, aren't you, Pete?"

"I'd feel just as bad if you were in the hands of kidnapers," I retorted.

Kittie's eyes filled with tears. "I hope so, but I doubt it,"
she said.

In half an hour, Captain Mullins came in, puffing. He
was twenty pounds overweight, but I think he had lost a
few pounds since the Ray trouble started.

"Where is it?" he asked eagerly. I pointed. Mullins
yanked off the paper wrapping and a square box was
revealed. He pulled off the cover and swore loudly.

"Nothing but a damned phonograph record," he growled.
He lifted it out of the box. It was a ten-inch record, obviously an amateur recording, since there was no company
brand or title on it.

"By Jove, a letter!" he exclaimed. There was a small envelope in the box beneath the record. He stuck his fat finger
under the flap and it came open without tearing. He pulled
out a folded sheet of letter paper and began to read. As he
read his eyes glittered and he almost turned purple with
excitement.

"What's it about?" I asked, without much interest. I couldn't get up much interest in anything.

He thrust it under my nose. He was almost smoking with excitement.

"Know that writing?" he demanded. I got excited. It was a round, boyish and familiar script—Ronnie Ray's.

"Ray," I said curtly, and I read the letter:

My dear Lita:

I know you are frightfully distressed by the reports of my death and until now I've had no chance to let you know that they are not true. A horrible thing has happened. I had to clear out, and until certain things work out I can't show my nose. I'm awfully sorry on your account as well as my own, because it has thrown you out of employment. I'm sending you positive proof that I'm alive and well, a record I've just made. The machine wasn't very good but if you are still in doubt you'll not doubt when you hear my voice.

Ronnie.

"So it was him you and Miss Bond saw on Bear Mountain!" Mullins exclaimed.

"Put that record on," I said hoarsely. I pointed to the big radio phonograph which has to be included in the furnishings of a modern advertising agency office.

HE PUT THE record on. Frankly, I was so shaken I couldn't get out of my chair. In a couple of seconds the room was filled with a voice, and there was no other voice like it in the world.

The thing gave me the horrors. I didn't know the number, but I knew that voice. It had been made on one of the machines which enable you to do your own recording, and while it was uneven and almost faded out once or twice—oh, it was Ronnie Ray!

The door to Kittie's office flew open. She stood inside, pale and trembling, until the record ended on a beautiful high note.

"Well," said Captain Mullins after a second, "what does it prove? He could have made it months ago."

Kittie dropped into a chair—pale as a phantom.

"I heard that song last night," she said. "It's 'I'll Love You Forever,' from the new revue, 'Handsome Is as Handsome Does.' The show only opened three nights ago. The music has only just been published. Ronnie disappeared a month ago."

"Who published it?" asked Mullins. "Marks and Marks," she said. "Wooster bought me a copy last night."

"Couldn't Ray have got an advance copy?" asked the captain.

"Wait," said Kittie. She ran out of the room. Mullins and I sat looking at each other for five minutes without saying a word. Kittie came back looking as though she were going to faint.

"The song is an interpolated number," she said. "It was only written three weeks ago. It was put into the show on the opening night in New York. They did a rush job in publishing it. Received it from Steve Blue, the composer, two weeks ago. Marks and Marks say that hit numbers like that are guarded carefully in the publishing office."

"Ray has been dead four weeks, but he sings a song that was written after he was murdered. What does that spell, Hunter?" demanded the captain.

"He isn't dead," I said wearily. "And everything that has happened is a bad dream. Forman is alive and so is Iona Ivar, and I didn't kill Louie the Loup in self-defense, and Barbara is back in her home."

"This guy is going nuts," observed the police captain to Kittie. "It means that Ray is alive. In a fit of jealousy lest this Ivar woman succeed him on the radio he murdered her. He's alive and running amuck. Nobody but him wrote that card that was tied to the knife in the woman's heart. We'll round him up, and this time he'll really be electrocuted."

HE SEEMED QUITE pleased. "I'm taking this record along with me," he said. "Will the Commissioner be surprised!"

He put the record back in the box, placed the letter with it, and put on the box cover. Picking up the wrapper, he scrutinized the pest mark.

"Mailed day before yesterday at the Central Post Office. Same writing on the wrapper as in the letter. You identify the handwriting as well as the voice on the wrapper?"

"Oh, yes. I identify them," I said.

"Let me see the letter," demanded Kittie. She read it rapidly.

"I know his writing. It's Ronnie," she said.

When we were alone we looked at each other. "Well?" Kittie said.

"It couldn't have been Ronnie I saw at the inn," I admitted. "I've seen him twice since, and here's a letter and a record of a song that was written after he was killed. Only, I just can't believe it."

"You made Ronnie," she reflected. "Yet he and his companions try desperately to kill you. Ronnie was madly in love with Barbara, but he lures her into the hands of kidnapers. Pete, I'm a pretty good judge of men. I didn't think Ronnie Ray would harm a fly."

"He's a tool in their hands, of course."

She nodded. "Of course. Oh, why don't the police do something!"

"I can't stand much more, Kittie."

"Poor dear, with his crown of snow white hair," she said, smiling. "I must call Wooster up. This confirms his theory absolutely."

"Smart fellow, Wooster," I said sullenly. "Seems to me he's paying too much attention to you."

"Well," replied Kittie, "I can use attentions from a nice man. I'm twenty-three years old, and I don't want to be an old maid."

"Bah—"

But Kittie had gone back to her den.

When I was ready to leave the office extras were out. A boy waved a paper under my nose. The headline said:

RONALD RAY ALIVE BUT INSANE
WANTED FOR THE IONA IVAR MURDER.

18

THE CALL FROM BARBARA

AT EIGHT THIRTY that night I was playing blackjack with Bill Watts, the cop on duty in my apartment, when my phone rang.

"Take a collect charge from Miss Barbara Bond?" asked the operator. "Calling from Millford, New York."

"Put her on quick," I shouted.

In a moment she spoke. "Peter!" she cried. "Come and get me! I got away. I'm hiding!"

"Where are you?"

"In the Millford railroad station. I broke a window. The station was locked up. I'm in a pay station."

"You bet. Where's Millford?"

"I don't know. I've run ten miles across country. I'm hiding in an old barn. I'll be looking for you."

"What happened? Where's Ronnie?"

"I don't know. I didn't see him again. They blindfolded me and stuck tape over my mouth. A man was going to kill me, but I got away. I'm horribly frightened. How long will it take you?"

"I'll have to find out where the place is. I'll come at once. I'll stop at the station and honk five times. Oh, Barbara, it's wonderful—"

But the connection broke off and presently the operator said:

"The party has hung up."

"Well, well!" said my bodyguard. "And where are you going now?"

"Millford. I've got to find out where it is. That was Barbara Bond. She has escaped."

"I never heard of the place," said the cop.

But I was pulling an atlas out of the bookcase. Millford was a village on the Lackawanna in Orange County, New York, very close to both New Jersey and Pennsylvania. It wasn't very far from the New Jersey lakes—thirty or forty miles.

"You ain't leaving without talking to Captain Mullins," said my policeman. "You know what almost happened to you the last time. Call him up."

I hesitated. A lot of help the police had been the last time! However, if I didn't talk to Mullins, Watts would. I phoned him at his house.

"Wait a minute, I got to think," he said. "Are you game to be the fall-guy again?"

"I've got to go," I said excitedly.

"Okay. I'll get the state police. I'll have them block every road round Millford and stop every car. You'll be the only one let in. Maybe she's escaped, and maybe there is a guy with a gun against the back of her head. It's fifty or sixty miles by any road. By the time you get there you'll be safe-guarded as much as possible. Take along a gun of your own, though."

"Okay," I said, and hung up. Ten minutes later, with Policeman Watts's cannon in my pocket, I drove my roadster as fast as I dared toward the Holland Tunnel. The shortest way was to cut across a corner of Jersey.

For the third time I was starting out in the night for a rendezvous with death. The first time I had no premonition. Kittie was with me and we were following Barbara. The second time Barbara had driven—insanely—death from a bullet had missed me by an inch. And now I was alone. Of course there was the cordon of state police... A bullet flies faster than a motorcycle, I thought with a shudder. Maybe they would be in time and maybe not... if it was a trap....

And as I plunged across marshes and darted through Jersey towns I believed more and more that this was a deliberate scheme to get me. I knew they wanted my life. They'd made three attempts on it. Even the dauntless Barbara would say what she was told to say with a gun against the back of her neck. I was a fool. I could still turn back.

On the other hand, I'd been offered a chance. I had to take it, as Barbara had had to take the chance that Ronnie was not a corpse but a captive awaiting ransom. A girl as resourceful as she might have gotten away and be hiding in a barn, penniless, footsore, dependent on me.

Don Quixote, otherwise Peter Hunter, advertising agent! Swivel-chair cowboy, the world's worst shot! Bull luck had enabled me to hit my antagonist the other night and get away with my life. This time—

And yet, these rats would have underestimated Barbara. To them she was a pretty, slim, blond girl, as yellow as her hair. She might have gotten away....

I glanced at my speedometer and slowed up. I had ticked

seventy, and high speed in a motor car makes me nervous. I dropped to fifty and in a couple of minutes was up to sixty again.

I knew what Kittie would say about this. Sane, sensible, shrewd Kittie Ketchum. She'd say:

"Why didn't you send the police? If you weren't crazy about Barbara you'd let the police rescue her."

But Mullins wanted me to go in. Of course, to Mullins I was a decoy duck. The chief of the homicide squad would cheerfully swap my life for the persons of the bandits. I was useful to him.

By and by I had to stop to read roadside signs. I'd picked out a route from the roadbook, but at night it's so easy to take a wrong turn. Fortunately it wasn't raining, as it had been that first night, but there was no moon and the stars gave little illumination. And I had come to a region of unlighted roads.

I had plenty of time for thought during that long ride, and I was plenty frightened. Somebody once said that the hero is not the man who knows no fear, but the fellow whose heart is in his boots and yet goes over the top. I must be a real hero, because I was petrified with fear and yet I hopped up the car to sixty-five miles an hour down a dark, narrow road.

I DIDN'T KNOW I was nearing Millford until I heard a rattle behind me and saw a star in the road—a motorcycle headlight. It came on fast and suddenly was beside me.

"Pull up," snapped a state policeman. I braked and came to a stop within a hundred feet or so.

He threw his flashlight into my face. "Name?" he snapped.

"Peter Hunter."

"You answer the description, and so does the car," he said.

"How far am I from Millford?"

"Eight miles. You'll be stopped once or twice more. Fire one shot and you'll bring in twenty of us. All roads are guarded."

"Okay, brother."

"Say!" said the cop. "You've got lots of nerve, Hunter. Best of luck. If they get you, we'll get them. This village is surrounded."

I nodded. If he wanted to think I had lots of nerve that was all right. I got going again and he turned back.

Two miles further along another motor cop stopped me and passed me on. Nothing further happened. No cars showed behind and none passed me. In about ten minutes I passed a house, then another, and presently crossed a railroad track. The road turned right and I traveled with it. And then, isolated and dark, I saw a small railroad station. It wasn't more than half past eleven, but Millford was a deserted village.

It took nerve to stop beside the railroad station. I pulled out the police revolver and cocked it and then I thumped my horn, five short barks. Nothing happened.

A minute passed. Then a figure came out of some bushes on the left of the road and into the range of my headlights, a female figure in black. Her yellow hair, unloosed, was streaming behind. It was Barbara.

I was out of the car. She came running and threw herself into my arms. They closed round her tight.

"Oh, Peter, Peter, you darling," she sobbed. "Oh, Peter, how I've suffered!"

I lifted her into the car and climbed in beside her.

"Where are they? Are they around?" I asked.

"I haven't seen anybody at all. I've been buried in hay in a barn over there." She pointed to the left into the darkness.

Gosh, I felt good! "I think we ought to have an escort back," I said. I stuck my revolver out of the car and pulled the trigger. The report sounded as loud as a six-inch gun. Barbara screamed, and buried her face in my shoulder.

"Oh, they'll get me!" she cried wildly.

"Not a chance," I said loftily. "Local boy makes good."

I was so happy I was gibbering. A minute passed and then I saw three motorcycle headlights coming down the road. I glanced in the mirror and two headlights had appeared behind us. Then I did feel safe. In a few seconds we were surrounded by motorcycle cops who were peering into the car.

"It's all right," I told them. "This is Miss Bond, boys. How about an escort home?"

They broke into excited congratulations. They turned flashlights on Barbara and she lifted her head and smiled at them. Well, I suspect that there are now five motorcycle cops who don't think as much of their wives and sweethearts as they did. Barbara Bond, pale, disheveled, in a dress that was torn and rent, was ravishingly beautiful.

They began to ask questions.

"I can't talk now," she said. "Please don't ask me."

"But we've got to round them up. Can you lead us to the place?"

"I don't know where it is. I walked and ran for hours in half a dozen different directions. I've had no sleep—"

"I'm taking this girl home, boys," I said. "She got away from some place within a radius of ten miles, and that's all she knows."

A car came roaring along from the rear and drew up beside us. Out jumped Captain Mullins, the commissioner of police, and Wooster Williams. We had the questions over again, but they did no good. Barbara had laid her head on my shoulder and fallen fast asleep.

A couple of more motorcycles drove up. One of them was ridden by the chief of the state police.

AFTER A CONFERENCE between the big wigs the New York Police commissioner came over. "Better take her home," he said. "We'll comb the countryside within a radius of twenty miles. We've forty men within call. In the morning we'll want her to identify suspects. I'll send a couple of motorcycles to escort you."

And so I drove back the way I had come. Half an hour passed while the girl lay motionless against me. Thrilling me—why wouldn't it? She was wrapped in a greatcoat provided by the police commissioner.

Suddenly Barbara quivered, pulled away, sat up straight and smiled at me.

"I'm all right now," she said. "You must be awfully tired. Why not let me drive?"

"I rode with you at the wheel once," I told her firmly. "Never again. You'll be a passenger and like it."

"A-a-a-ll r-r-right," she murmured, and fell over against me, sound asleep again. What a girl!

Barbara's big house was a blaze of lights when we drove

up. The police had phoned in the good news and all the servants were waiting. The door flew open and the butler and the housekeeper, a couple of footmen and three maids rushed down the steps, but I carried Barbara in myself and took her upstairs to the bedroom indicated by the butler. As I laid her down she opened her eyes and went into a paroxysm of coughing.

"Call her doctor, quick," I commanded. I sat by her, but she was unconscious again. In five minutes the doctor came in and put me out.

When I got back to my apartment Officer Watts grinned at me.

"You got more lives than a cat," he said, "Where's my gat?"

I handed it over. He examined it. "One shot fired. Whom did you kill?"

"Oh, I fired it to start a motorcycle race," I told him. After that I called up Kittie, who was in bed, and told her the good news. Naturally she was delighted, but she bawled me out for the chance I took.

"The police could have rescued her just as well," she declared.

"Barbara preferred me," I said proudly. "And I brought home the bacon."

"She wouldn't care to be called 'bacon,'" Kittie came back, and hung up on me. Kittie could be kind of mean on occasion.

19

THE SUPERSTITIOUS TENOR

I WAS EATING my ham and eggs in my bedroom at nine o'clock the next morning when in walked Wooster Williams.

"What luck?" I demanded eagerly.

"None," he said gloomily. "The whole business was muddled up. They should have made the girl describe the place where she was a captive. We didn't have a thing to go on."

"You had a ten-mile radius," I told him, "in a thinly settled country. Excuse me. I'm calling up to find out how Miss Bond is feeling."

"You can't talk to her. Nobody can. She's down with pneumonia."

"Good God!"

He nodded gloomily. "The state police rounded up a few suspicious-looking characters, and wanted her to look them over. There are three doctors up there and about six nurses. It may be a couple of weeks before she can tell us what happened."

"So she should have been forced to talk last night," I said furiously. "In which case she might be dead today."

"I don't believe she would be any worse off. Hunter, we might have nabbed the gang."

"I understand your point of view."

I told him sarcastically.

"Did she say anything to you at all?"

"No, she was asleep—I suppose it was a stupor—all the way home. But she said over the phone that she never saw Ronnie after that glimpse of him in the road."

Williams walked up and down the room, his hands in his pockets.

"The man's conduct is inexplicable," he burst out. "Ray could have married the girl and had millions. He robs her of two hundred thousand, which he has to divide with his confederates. The police believe that he killed Iona Ivar out of jealousy. That would mean that he is a homicidal maniac. He sends Miss Lawton that transcription to prove that he is alive. He writes a lot of hooey about the predicament he finds himself in—"

"Find Miss Lawton, why don't you?"

"Every effort by state, local and Federal officials is being made to find the damn woman! Here's an impractical musician, a little old maid of a pianist, and she baffles the nation."

"You know, of course, that she is not a dummy. She deliberately faked dumbness—"

"Yes, I know that— By God!"

"What?" I demanded.

He smashed his fist on the table. "Maybe she killed Iona Ivar! We've learned little or nothing about her past. Ivar turns up with knowledge of her. Maybe information that reflects on her. We know she is cunning and crafty—"

"You're a great detective," I jeered. "I suppose that poor little old maid, for whom all the police of the nation are searching, walked into a hotel, let herself into a locked room, and murdered Iona Ivar and made a getaway, leaving no clue. Yeah!"

He laughed good-naturedly. "You don't think much of me, Hunter. I look like an unlicked cub, of course, and you don't know anything about my accomplishments. I have a habit of thinking out loud and a lot of my thoughts are wild. I let my imagination run riot, and you'd be surprised what results it sometimes brings me. The other day you laughed in my face when I told you I thought Ray was alive."

"Well, it looks as though you were right. I apologize."

"Don't bother. I'm not as sure as I was."

"What? With the record of a song written after he was supposed to be dead."

"I'm wondering about that. Why the anxiety to persuade Miss Lawton that he's still alive? He has no further use for the woman. He can't come back to radio after his participation in the kidnaping of Miss Bond."

"If he proves that he was forced to—"

"We know there are people who want it believed that he is alive. Suppose they cooked up this record? Handwriting can be forged."

"Stay put somewhere, will you?" I objected. "I know Ronnie Ray's voice. He made that record."

"There may be another voice exactly like it."

"In which case the owner can make five thousand a week by applying at my office, Williams. You can't forge a voice, young fellow."

"Say, I've heard Caruso records, and I've heard others with a voice just like his," William argued. "All good singers sound alike."

"I don't believe you're any judge.

"It's said by experts that there never was a voice like Caruso's before him or since. And that goes for Ronnie Ray's. It has a peculiar quality which is unmistakable."

He picked up his hat. "Take care of yourself. I'm going down South."

"I thought the government never dropped a case," I wisecracked.

"I'm not dropping it. Miss Bond, who could tell us all about these bandits, can't talk for at least a couple of weeks. I think this Ivar woman must have left a broad trail. I'm going as far back on it as I can get."

"Why?"

He laughed. "Haven't got time to tell you. Good-by."

HE WAS GONE like a flash. I shrugged my shoulders. Good thing. Kittie would probably miss Kim, but she was seeing too much of him. I took a fatherly interest in Kittie. And why wouldn't I? She had come to me from business college, just a kid, and she was a swell girl. It would be a mistake for a girl like Kittie to marry a guy in a business that made his prospects of getting his head blown off pretty certain. I'd read a few days before about two Department of Justice operators who had been murdered by bank robbers, and there was poor old Forman, stabbed to death in my other twin bed. And Forman had twice as much on the ball as this fellow.

I was getting ready to leave when Kittie phoned.

"Duplon just called up," she said. "He wants you to buy

him Locatelli of the Metropolitan. He'll pay the price. He says he and Madame have agreed not to fool with any more unknowns. The business requires a big name."

"Did you tell him Locatelli will cost, at least three thousand a broadcast?"

"Yes, he says he'll pay that."

"He's getting some sense," I said. "I'll stop at Locatelli's hotel on the way downtown."

Locatelli was a great Italian lyric tenor who had been a sensation for two years at the Metropolitan. He had just finished twenty broadcasts for a motor car company, one of my clients, but the company had gone broke, despite the popularity of the broadcast, because it had gambled everything on a freak car that everybody laughed at and nobody would buy. The bankruptcy was going to cost the Hunter Agency fifty thousand a year, and it left Locatelli at liberty.

He lived in a select side-street hotel in the Fifties near Fifth Avenue. I arrived there in half an hour and sent up my name. He phoned down to have me come up.

He was a short, fat young man with curling black hair and big black eyes and a very pleasant smile. He greeted me warmly. He was wearing a red brocade dressing gown, most unbecoming, but he enjoyed it.

"Meester 'Unter," he exclaimed. "An honor! What can I get you? A big drink? *Si?*"

"A big drink, no. I don't indulge in the morning. I have a swell job for you, Locatelli. Three grand a broadcast."

"Ah, that is wonderful! How many?"

"You're likely to keep going for years on this one."

He clapped his hands and grinned from ear to ear.

"Who is the sponsor, eh?"

"Perfumes of Arcady."

His expression changed. His mouth fell open. He turned pea-green. He held out his right hand with his first two fingers crossed.

"*Ah, non, non!*" he cried. "Never! Not me! Get someone else!"

"Are you nuts? How many sponsors will pay your price?"

"Not for ten thousand dollars. Twenty. Nevair!"

"Why?"

"Because these perfumes, they unlucky. I am young. I wish to live," he shouted.

"Why, you blithering idiot—"

He shook his fist at me. "You do not tempt me. *Non!* Ronnie Ray—he is dead This Iona Ivar, she is dead! Now you want to make me dead! I say, nevair!"

"Don't you read the papers? Ray is alive!"

"I think he is not. The beeg fat womans—"

"She wasn't engaged for Perfumes of Arcady."

"Then why warn her she must not sing for them?" he shouted.

"Locatelli, I ought to know. I engaged her. I wanted her for another program," I said.

"*Si?* Then it is you and your agency that is unlucky. Two deaths. They go in threes. Nothing is doing, Meester 'Unter."

"Well, the deuce with you," I said thoroughly exasperated. "The world is full of good singers."

"Let them die, not me."

I slammed the door upon the superstitious Italian, but I grew very thoughtful as I went downstairs. Most musicians are superstitious. It was going to be a fine state of affairs if I couldn't hire anybody at any price! It meant Duplon's ruin, and I'd crash along with him, probably. Let the fools get the notion that the agency was unlucky... Oh, Lord, what next?

20

TWO PHOTOGRAPHS

I CALLED BARBARA'S house and talked with the butler, who told me that she had pneumonia, but was resting easily, and that the doctors were very hopeful. Feeling a little better I went on to the office and told Kittie about Locatelli.

"The idiot," she said angrily. "He'll give us a bad name."

"It's a darn serious situation," I said, wagging my head. After that I had to go all over the experience of the past night, and she grew excited.

"This time I took no risk whatever," I assured her.

"Well, see that you don't take any more. Wooster called up. He's taking a plane for Baltimore. May be gone a week."

"Which is tough on you."

She laughed. "He's really very nice and very clever, but I can get along. Before we get any more turndown by tenors, I'm going over to call on Madame Duplon. We can get a company of actors and do the mystery playlets with the perfume angle that I told you about, for one quarter what Locatelli would cost. There's no use in talking to Duplon— he's only an echo of Madame. And I really believe that no singer will deliver for Perfumes after Ronnie. People wouldn't want to tune in. The thing is an entirely different sort of program. We can get people to write the scripts easily enough.

"Put it over, Kittie, and you get a bonus."

"I don't think this office can stand any bonuses," she replied. "Pete don't worry about Barbara. That girl has the constitution of a horse. She'll be all right."

"Well, if you'd seen the poor kid last night—"

"I know. I'm off to see Madame Duplon."

I made up my mind, then and there, that I would give Kittie an interest in the business, assuming we had a business after what we were going through.

She came back in the middle of the afternoon, smiling.

"Put it over," she said. "Madame and I cried about Ronnie. She's still in love with him, and if he ever comes back he returns to the Perfume Hour. In the meantime, we organize the 'Perfumes of Arcady' dramatic company. I'm going to send out a call for radio authors. It will take a week to prepare scripts."

"Good girl," I approved.

Nothing happened that night, for a wonder. Kittie and I went to a show after dinner, and I and my shadows saw her home and then I went to bed. And the following morning there was good news. Barbara was conscious, but wouldn't talk. The doctor said that she wanted to see me and I could have ten minutes with her the following morning.

"I won't have her pestered by police," he said over the phone. "Officially she has pneumonia. Actually, she was chilled and exhausted, but has almost recovered now. It will be three or four days before I'll let any flatfoot see her."

"That's right, doctor. I'll keep mum."

"I'll phone you at nine tomorrow morning if she's strong

enough," the doctor went on. "She has pleurisy, which is bad enough, and we can't take any chances."

"You bet we can't," I said joyfully. Hardly had I hung up when the phone rang again. It was the police commissioner's secretary.

"The chief wants to see you at ten-thirty," he said. "Very important."

"Okay, I'll be there," I answered.

The commissioner was a good fellow and as considerate as they make them, but I was fed up with questions. All I wanted to do was to get Ronald Ray out of my mind and get some constructive business ideas. I phoned the office that I would be late, as usual, and at ten-thirty I was waiting in the commissioner's office.

"Sorry to keep pestering you, Hunter," he said, "but you're the crux of this situation. How is Miss Bond?"

"Just the same," I said shortly.

"It's a pity. I've a couple of interesting matters to discuss with you. Do you recognize these photographs?"

He had taken from his desk two unmounted prints, and I stared at them in astonishment.

"Looks like Ronnie. Don't flatter him, though," I said.

"These are pictures of one Arthur Clarkson," said the commissioner." I have also Clarkson's finger-prints and Bertillon measurements. Unfortunately it's too late to check up on the body you found in Jersey. It is far gone."

"You mean Ronnie's name is Clarkson. But we know everything about him—"

"Clarkson was tried and convicted and sent to state prison in Indiana for cracking a safe. He got fifteen years.

Was put away in 1929. He escaped in a general break in 1932."

"But we know that Ronnie—"

"WE HAVEN'T A trace of Ray from 1927 until two years ago, when he came into notice as a radio singer," the commissioner pointed out. "He was discharged from a shoe store uptown in 1927. In his letter to Miss Lawton he spoke of a horrible situation which caused him to disappear. Mightn't it be that he was recognized by a fellow convict? It's even possible that he knocked out the man who recognized him, dressed him in his own clothes, and electrocuted him."

I laughed at that.

"The other 'con' must have been his twin brother," I objected. "The idea is too far-fetched."

The commissioner nodded.

"If Ronnie was capable of murdering a man in that way he had guts enough to go right on with his broadcasting," I argued.

"No, he wanted it believed that it was he who was killed."

"How come this escaped convict sang on the radio and had a thousand pictures of himself in newspapers without those Hoosier cops identifying him?" I asked.

"Studio pictures are so touched up and so flattering that they are deceptive, Besides, the Indiana police wouldn't expect to find an escaped convict in Ronald Ray, the most famous radio singer of the day. Wooster Williams, however, sent pictures of Ray to every prison and police headquarters in the country, having a theory that Ray's curious behavior—Williams believes he is alive—was due to a criminal past. Looks as though he was right. His theory brought out these photographs."

"Well," I said with a sigh, "Ronnie didn't look to me like a burglar, but I'm getting so I'll believe anything."

"Now, on the other hand," the commissioner said, "assuming that it was Ray who was murdered in Jersey, isn't it possible that it is Clarkson whom you and Miss Bond saw the night she was captured, and whom you saw in the subway train? We know that this—shall we say apparition—is associating with criminals and murderers. Well, Clarkson is a criminal."

"Now, you're talking!" I exclaimed. "Sure! That's the explanation."

"But there remains the voice which sang 'Barbara Allen' to Miss Bond over the phone, and the voice which made the record of a revue number which was written after Ray was supposed to be dead."

"I can't explain that," I said wearily.

"And I've talked with the state prison in Indiana this morning. The warden says that they have a choir there and draft prisoners who can sing, but that Clarkson was not a singer so far as he knows."

"So we're back where we started from," I summed up.

"Some progress. We know that either Ray or his double was an escaped convict named Clarkson. And you had no difficulty observing a strong resemblance in these pictures to Ray."

"It looks like him, but Ronnie had a frank, open expression. This guy looks crafty."

"Ray was on top of the world. That may account for the

difference. Have you had any communication from Miss Lawton?"

"No, nothing."

"Well, I'm much obliged to you, Mr. Hunter."

I left headquarters with plenty to think about.

21

BARBARA'S ESCAPE

"HOW IS MISS Bond?" I asked the butler eagerly when he admitted me.

"She's very much better, sir," he replied. "In two or three days she will be all right, but we are telling everybody that her condition is unchanged. Doctor's orders."

"Quite right. The doctor says I may see her."

"Yes, Mr. Hunter. This way, sir."

He led me up the wide marble stair. The house was a palace, built by her father, the late Henry Stewart Bond. He was dead and his daughter had an income of millions a year to spend—and how she had spent them.

The butler conducted me to the huge bedroom at the rear of the house into which I had carried Barbara. He opened the door. I was shaking with excitement when he opened the door. There was a white-robed nurse standing beside the window and the whiskered doctor sat in a chair beside the bed. He rose and bowed. Barbara was sitting up against lace pillows, pale but beautiful.

She smiled and lifted her right hand to me.

"Ten minutes, Mr. Hunter," said the doctor. "She mustn't get tired. She insists upon seeing you in private."

"Go away, please," said Barbara in a very hoarse voice. "I'm all right."

"Ten minutes only," warned the physician.

He filed out with the nurse, and the door closed behind them.

Barbara grinned at me. "Hello," she said. "Am I hoarse!"

It was a statement, not a question.

"Don't strain your voice, dear," I said and sat down in the chair vacated by the physician.

"Pneumonia, laugh that off," she requested. "I caught a cold on my chest and I was utterly exhausted. Dr. Rawson is a nice man, but an old fogy. He jumped at conclusions and didn't even make the pneumonia tests until yesterday, when I insisted. You see I was very weak and the cold racked me. Much obliged, Peter, for the other night."

"I'm so happy to think—"

"I'd let you kiss me only you might take my cold."

So I kissed her. Then I said, "We have only ten minutes. I want to hear—"

"Oh, I had a perfectly horrible time, Peter. It was dreadful. I'll begin at the beginning. I stepped out of the car at the same time you did. The man called, 'Ronnie, come here.' I was off guard. Then two shots rang out. Peter, the man, hit me in the forehead with the butt of his revolver. When I came to I was in the back seat of the car, wedged between two men. There was a bandage around my eyes and tape over my mouth and my hands were tied in back and my ankles were tied.

"The car was traveling fast. My first thought was that I had caused your death by bringing you with me, and I was horribly distressed. I knew I had been tricked again, and that it couldn't be Ronnie I had seen because it would mean that he was one of this gang of criminals. I knew you believed he was dead and that there was a double posing for him, and I felt then that you were right. I couldn't speak or move. Nobody in the car said a word, but there seemed to be somebody groaning in the bottom of the car, on the floor."

"That was the brute I shot."

"I know. I learned afterward. Well, we drove for hours before we stopped. I was lifted out and carried into a house and placed on a bed with a very hard mattress. They left me bound, gagged and blindfolded on that bed, Peter. All night. Nobody came near me."

"You poor child!"

"I could tell when it was daylight, of course. After a long time a man came in and sat on the edge of the bed. He yanked at the tape on my mouth and took a lot of skin off my lips.

" 'Miss Bond,' he said, 'we want more money.'

" 'Where is Ronnie?' I exclaimed.

" 'Tied up as you are, in another room,' he said. 'Poor devil, he feels terrible at being forced to help us capture you.'

" 'You have the money. Let us go.'

"He laughed. 'Oh, we want much more money,' he told me. 'We want half a million for the two of you.'

" 'Try to get it!'

" 'We'll get it or you and Ray will be killed out of hand,' he said. He sounded very merciless. Of course I couldn't see what he looked like, and somehow, Peter, I didn't believe a word about Ronnie being a fellow-captive. I believed that he was dead, that he was the dead man you found.

" 'You'll have to let me go to get money from me,' I told him.

" 'You'll find a way to get it from here,' he came back.

" 'My good man,' I said, 'My fortune is in the hands of a bank. I haven't a father or mother to ransom me. And my kidnaping is known, so no check of mine will be cashed. Take this bandage off my eyes.'

" 'NOTHING DOING. You will write five checks for a hundred thousand dollars, dating them tomorrow. You'll give your word that they'll be cashed when you're released. I know a lot about you. If you give your word even to criminals, you'll keep it. You'll promise not to tip the police.'

" 'And you'll let Ronnie go with me?' I asked.

" 'He stays here until the money is safe in our hands.'

" 'You'll let me go on my word?'

" 'Yes.'

" 'You don't get it, you devil!' I cried. 'You're lying! I don't believe that man is Ronald Ray.'

" 'You know he is.'

" 'Anyway, there isn't a chance in the world of these checks being cashed, even if I okay them,' I exclaimed.

" 'They will go through the bank as a legitimate business transaction—payment of securities delivered to you,' he said. 'We have it all worked out.'

" 'I'll stay here till I rot!' I screamed. I was so wildly angry at being tricked and so nervous from my bonds and the bandage that I was willing to let them kill me rather than give in to them.

"The man got off the bed. 'Try rotting for a few days,'

he said. 'We're in no hurry. Would you like to have Ronnie sing to you?'

"Ronald Ray is dead and you know it!' I stormed. He didn't say anything but walked out of the room... Peter, in a minute, through the walls came Ronnie's voice, singing 'Barbara Allen.'"

"Barbara, it couldn't—" I began.

"It was his voice. Don't I know it," Barbara insisted. "But somehow, it didn't move me. If he loved me he wouldn't have stepped in front of the car and lured me into stopping. You saw him smile and wave his hand. It came to me that he was a weak, worthless creature. If it had been I, I'd let them shoot me before I'd betray somebody I loved. I said to myself, 'Well, he got me into this. Let him get me out, if he's a man.'"

"You don't love him any more?" I demanded.

"I stopped loving him when that man hit me on the head with his revolver, I think. Isn't it funny how a girl can be deceived in a personality? There was a glamour around him because of his voice, but even when I asked him to marry me—I did, you know—I knew that he was a weakling."

"Never mind. Go on," I said.

"I just gritted my teeth and listened to the song. The man stuck his head in the door and said, 'Well?'

" 'Nothing doing, damn you,' I screamed at him. 'And tell that idiot I don't want to hear any more singing.' He slammed the door.

"All that day I rubbed the rope around my wrists against the edge of the wire spring on the cot I was laying on, and finally, toward night I fell asleep. They didn't give me anything to eat or drink, Peter."

"The filthy brutes!" I exclaimed.

"In the morning the man stuck his head in the door, and I swore at him. All that day I kept rubbing, rubbing. The ropes were half an inch thick, but I was gradually wearing them through. The man came in and gave me a glass of water in the afternoon. Two days without food! I had strength enough to laugh at him, and he went off swearing."

"You're incredible, Barbara."

She nodded and smiled. "I have will power. About the middle of that night, the bonds on my wrists parted. I whipped off the bandage. I unfastened the ropes around my ankles. When I stood up I fell on the floor from exhaustion. There was no light in the room, but I felt my way to the window. Everything was black outside. I tried the window, but it was nailed down and a dog began to bark outside. It sounded like a big fierce dog. I went back to the bed and fell asleep, now that the bonds didn't irk me.

"I woke quite late. I fastened the ropes around my ankles again and put on the bandage and then laid the ropes around my wrists. If they came in and found out I was loose, they would tie me up tight. In the afternoon the man gave me a glass of water. I tried to peer at him from under the bandage, but I couldn't see him.

" 'Give in?' he asked.

" 'No, damn you?' I shouted.

" 'You 'will,' he said with a nasty laugh. About dusk I heard a car drive away, and a little while afterwards the door opened suddenly. I had pushed the bandage up so I could see under it and I saw a man enter. He came over and stood beside the bed. He was a small, dark man, very mean looking.

"To my horror, he suddenly drew a knife from his pocket.

" 'I'll put a stop to this,' he said in a thin, sharp voice. And he lifted up the knife, Peter."

"Good God!"

"I DREW UP my knees and drove both feet against his stomach and he went flying backward. I threw off the rope around my wrists, but had no time to untie my feet, for he was up and coming for me. I pushed off the bandage and grasped his right wrist with both hands. I twisted it until the knife fell out of his hand and then I shook him like a rat and grasped his throat and we went down on the floor. Weak as I was, I was stronger than he, and I kept squeezing his throat until he stopped kicking and clawing at me and lay still.

"Then I ran to the door. It was open. I stumbled across a dark living room; found the outside door, which was unlocked, and ran outside. There were woods all around. A big dog came barking at me and I kicked him. He was a mongrel and ran away, and I rushed into the woods.

"I kept running. Sometimes I had to stop to rest. I got out of the woods and blundered into a swamp. It came up to my knees but I got through it and kept going. That's how I got my cold. I suppose I went around in circles, but I kept going for hours. I never saw a house with a light in it, though I passed several that were boarded up, summer places.

"I was about through when I saw a house with lights, but I was afraid to go up to it. I didn't know but it was the place I had escaped from. And then I hit a highroad and a railroad track, and came upon the railroad station. There was an old barn across the road and I thought the best thing to do was to telephone to you. Oh, the man had told me you got away. I asked and he said, 'He got away, damn him.'"

"If you hadn't answered, I would have called the New York police and asked them to come."

"But there must have been a police station in Millford. People would have taken you in," I said.

"I suppose I was out of my mind," she said. "I was horribly afraid and I was so weak I didn't think I could go a quarter of a mile further. I got into the depot and found the pay station and then I went over and hid in the barn. I guess I fell asleep, because the next thing I knew your horn was honking. I was never really afraid before, Peter, but those days without food took the courage out of me."

I drew a long breath. "I wonder if you know what an amazing person you are," I remarked. "After three days of starvation, you tackle a man with a knife and overpower him, choke him senseless—"

"He was a small man—"

She had a fit of coughing. Her voice had been growing more hoarse with each sentence. And at that minute the doctor and nurse returned wearing determined expressions. I rose.

"May I see her tomorrow?" I asked.

"If you haven't worn her out today," he promised.

"You be sure to come tomorrow," commanded Barbara.

"Could you recognize the place again—"

"You must go, Mr. Hunter," said the doctor sternly.

Barbara shook her head. "It was dark and I was so frightened."

With that I had to leave. My admiration for the girl was boundless, of course. She ought to have been a man. Such courage—after only twenty-four hours without food I personally would have agreed to anything.

I TOOK A taxi to the office and went carefully over what she had told me. It was evident that the car which had departed had carried off Ronnie and everybody except the man who had attempted to murder Barbara. Had they decided she would never give in and should be put out of the way? Had they left the assassin behind, or had he some personal hatred which had caused him to attack her with a knife?

The thing to do, of course, was to put the police into possession of what I had learned from Barbara. Delay might be an insurmountable handicap.

I sent for Captain Mullins, and he came running when he learned that I had Barbara's statement. He made notes of everything I said and made no comment until I had finished.

"That's the most remarkable young woman I ever heard of," he said. "And it means there is dissension in the ranks of the bandits. This fellow with the knife was double-crossing the others. They wouldn't kill the girl who might bring them half a million. They left this crazy man in charge of her and he couldn't resist the opportunity to commit murder."

"She says positively that it was Ronnie who was singing in the next room," I reminded him. "Looks like he's alive."

"The worst of this case is we can't get a motive for anything they do. What in God's name is his motive?"

"Well, I've told you all I know," I reminded him.

"I suppose she'd recognize the room she was confined

in," he said thoughtfully. "We'll comb that district again, and when she's well enough we'll have her look over a few places."

"What good will that do? It's probably a summer cottage that they took possession of."

"Sure, but if they were there for several days they might have left something that will give us a clue."

Mullins went off and then I had to tell the whole story to Kittie.

"Looks like you're in right," she said. "She's disgusted with Ronnie and she'll nab you on the rebound. You've got a chance, Peter."

"She just considers me as a friend."

"No girl considers any young man as just a friend," Kittie retorted. "Think of all her money, Peter."

"I'm not marrying any girl for her money."

"No, but it's nice to have, and if this business blows up she'll probably make you a liberal allowance."

"Kittie," I said angrily. "There are times when I'd like to sock you on the nose."

"The butler would probably treat you respectfully. Didn't you tell me once you always get seasick on yachts."

"Miss Ketchum," I said severely. "Take a letter."

"Okay," she grinned. "Let's see if you can concentrate."

"Oh, clear out and leave me alone!" I shouted.

Kittie grinned in a more exasperating manner. "Yes, Mr. Hunter, sir," she answered, and with much dignity departed from my presence.

22

THE MYSTERIOUS BROADCAST

MADAME CLAIRE DUPLON was having her coffee in bed in the Hotel Warwick, into which she had moved her husband a year back when she became convinced that Perfumes of Arcady were going to make them multi-millionaires and she might as well stop scrimping and enjoy life. Madame had a maid and Duplon had a valet, and they had a six-thousand-dollar car upon the tire cover of which they had not been able to resist painting: *Perfumes of Arcady.*

About ten o'clock, as she remembered it, the phone rang and the maid answered it. "It is the International Broadcasting," the maid said. "A most important message for you, Madame."

She took the phone. "It is Madame Duplon in person," she said haughtily. "Why do you disturb me?"

"Listen in on International at ten-thirty. Greatly to your advantage."

It was a man's voice. Madame sputtered into the phone before she realized that he had hung up after that one speech and cut her off.

"Quick!" she commanded of the maid. "Get me up. I must get to the radio."

At ten-thirty Madame Duplon, much excited, sat in
front of the big machine in the living room of her suite. If
she made a discovery, it would be something to flaunt in
front of her husband and that conceited advertising agent,
meaning yours truly, Peter Hunter.

"First broadcast of Ramon Ranova, brilliant pianist—"

"*Chut!*" exclaimed Madame Duplon. "My time they
should take to listen to pianists."

"—in the latest revue hit, 'Love Me Forever,'" droned
the announcer. "Arranged by Mr. Ranova."

There was a crashing chord, and an introduction.
Madame's hand was on the radio switch. It dropped. A
voice lifted in song—a marvelous voice—a unique voice.

"Oh, *mon Dieu, mon Dieu!*" screamed Madame Duplon.
"Ronnie! It is Ronnie! He has come back, Marie, quick.
Listen!"

The song ended and the piano went into a florid number.
It was a number lasting several minutes. Again came the
lovely, the inimitable voice, and this time it sang "Barbara
Allen."

As Madame Duplon hadn't been taken into police
confidence she was not aware that this song was of special
significance to Barbara Bond. She listened entranced.

The broadcast ended. Madame was laughing and crying.

"I have found him!" she cried. "It is I who have found
him!" She rushed to the telephone and called my office.
Kittie answered.

"Quick, Keettie!" Madame cried. "I must talk to Peter!"

Kittie switched me on the line.

"Ronnie is back!" Madame yelled. "I hear him broadcast
just now from International—"

"Impossible," I said.

"Don't I believe my own ears?" she screamed. "Don't I know my darling's voice?"

"All right, all right. What time did he come on?"

"At ten-thirty," she screamed at me.

"Is he still singing?"

"No, it is over. I was entranced."

"Hold the line." I summoned Kittie. "Get International on another phone. Madame says Ray broadcasted from there at ten-thirty. It's now ten fifty-five."

"Why, they wouldn't—"

"Call them immediately."

I turned to my own phone.

"Madame," I said, "you mean to say that they announced a broadcast by Ronnie Ray, and then he sang?"

"No, they say some Spanish name—Ramon something—but I know Ronnie's voice."

"I'll get right up there. Thanks, Madame." I hung up on her. I had my hat and coat on when Kittie entered.

"Madame is cuckoo," she said, smiling. "They had a piano program at ten-thirty. Ramon Ranova—a sustaining period."

"I'm going up there," I told her, and left on the run. In ten minutes I burst into the offices of Aubrey Gray, broadcast manager at International.

"I want to know' all about your ten-thirty program," I demanded. "Artists, programs, everything."

"You look excited, Hunter. Have a chair. I don't know what the program was. I think it's a sustaining period. I'll find out."

He phoned his secretary.

"RAMON RANOVA, SPANISH pianist," he told me. "Brown, head of the music department, heard him ten days ago and gave him a tryout spot."

"Damn funny! Madame Duplon called me just now, greatly excited, and insisted that Ronald Ray was singing during that period."

He laughed loudly. "I hate to speak ill of a valuable client, but that old dame is crazy in the head."

"Like a fox," I muttered. "Get the announcer in here quick."

The announcer appeared in five minutes. He was a little man named Owens.

"You announced the Ranova piano program?" demanded Gray.

"Why, yes, Mr. Gray. Yes, indeed. Is anything wrong?"

"Was there any singing?" I asked eagerly.

"Why, yes. I was surprised myself, as it wasn't on my schedule, but Mr. Ranova sang two songs to his own accompaniment."

"What were the songs?" I shouted.

"One was 'I'll Love You Forever' with a very complicated and clever accompaniment, and the other was an English ballad. He didn't give me the name."

"Barbara Allen?" I demanded.

"Yes, that was it."

"Look here, did he sound like Ronnie Ray?"

"I'm not a good judge of voices, frankly; but now that you mention it, it was a baritone-tenor voice. There was a certain resemblance—"

"For God's sake get the sound man!" I demanded. "Hold this fellow!"

*"Don't touch those
drinks!" shouted
Williams*

In a couple of minutes the sound operator entered. Gray, by this time, was almost as excited as I was.

"You regulated the ten-thirty program?" demanded Gray. "Did this fellow's voice sound like Ronnie Ray's?"

The sound man nodded. "I was astonished. I worked with Ray a lot. It sounded very much like him."

"Did this fellow have permission to sing?" I demanded of Gray.

"Brown will know." He phoned.

"He offered a straight piano program. Modern and classic music," he reported.

I scratched my head. Madame hadn't told me that she had been notified to listen in. That was something I learned later.

"Something has been put over on you, but the purpose is beyond me," I observed. "Mr. Owens, what did this Ranova look like?"

"He was very dark, and not tall. I didn't pay any especial attention to him."

"Anybody with him?"

"There was another man, big fellow, looked like a Spaniard. He turned the music pages for him."

"You're sure the other man didn't do the singing?"

"Positive."

I was stumped.

"Call Ranova up," said Gray briskly. "The darn fool can't get a job that pays anything with his piano, but if he sings like Ray, he's got something we can sell. Duplon ought to be back on the air, Hunter. How about—"

"You'll never see this Ranova again," I said slowly. "This has some connection with the Ray mystery. Gray, please get hold of everybody who saw and talked with Ranova. I want a complete description of him. Get me his address. He won't be found there, but he may be traced."

"I don't see—"

"Neither do I," I said wearily. "I am wandering in the dark myself. But the police will want to talk with Ramon Ranova."

HE HAD THE address in a minute and I immediately called up Captain Mullins, told him the facts, and suggested grabbing the Spaniard.

"We'll go right after him," he said excitedly. "Thanks, old man."

"If he shows up 'round here again, nab him, Gray," I requested. "May I call Madame Duplon?"

"Certainly."

"Hunter speaking," I said when she answered. "I'm at International. Madame, it was not Ronnie you heard, but a Spaniard named Ramon Ranova. A small, dark man resembling Ronnie in no respect."

"Then why should I be called up and asked to listen in?" she demanded. "I tell you it was Ronnie!"

"This fellow has a voice very much like his, and he hopes you'll engage him. I can think of no other reason. So you were called up and told to listen in?"

"But certainly! Otherwise I would still be in bed. I think it most queer, *Monsieur* Hunter."

"I'm trying to locate Ranova. If you had only phoned as soon as you heard the voice we could have caught him at the studio."

"But I am entrance—so delighted—I weep for joy. I only call you when all is over."

"Well, it certainly wasn't Ronnie. I have these statements of the announcer and the sound man—"

Madame broke into sobs and I hung up on her.

"My office is full of people with appointments," said Gray pointedly.

Riding back to the office it suddenly struck me that the Ranova broadcast shed a glimmer of light in the darkness. The dark little man with the voice like Ronnnie's explained a lot. He had sung "Love Me Forever" and "Barbara Allen." That meant that it was Ranova who had made the record sent to Miss Lawton in care of my office. It meant that it was Ranova who had sung "Barbara Allen" over the phone to Barbara Bond.

Could it also mean that it was Ranova who had sung "Barbara Allen" in the next room to Barbara in the cottage near Millford? And was it Ranova who had attempted to murder Barbara as she Jay apparently bound and blindfolded on the cot in her prison? He was a small man, the would-be murderer. He was not strong, because Barbara had overpowered him.

And that meant that all the evidence produced to prove that Ronnie was alive was fabricated, worthless. His double couldn't sing. The double was Clarkson, the escaped convict from Indiana. His appearance, combined with Ronnie's voice, had deceived the police and befuddled Wooster Williams.

Ronald Ray, poor devil, was a decomposed corpse.

The mystery was almost as deep as ever, the motive of Ranova as inexplicable, but this idiotic broadcast had given us our first clue.

I told everything to Kittie when I reached the office, and she was as bewildered as I was.

"What do they expect to gain?" she demanded. "Why bother Madame Duplon?"

"By Jove, for the same reason that they killed poor Iona Ivar. They don't want us to put another artist on the Duplon broadcast."

"Yes, but why?"

"Well, I don't know why. Unless they have some reason for wishing to ruin Perfumes of Arcady. This Ranova is a killer. It's certain that he's the man who attacked Barbara with a knife," I declared.

"But Barbara couldn't have held out much longer. They expected to cash in—"

"I don't pretend to explain," I said. "The thing is, we know one of the criminals. We have a description of him. He's a pianist and a singer. That means that he's known by some of the concert or vaudeville agents. It won't be long now, Kittie, before the whole thing is cleared up."

"Why should Ranova want to murder you?" she demanded. "You never saw the man in your life. No such person was ever an applicant for work at this office, so you couldn't have turned him down."

"All I know is that I've a headache," I said testily.

"Why did Wooster have to go away? He's making something out of this."

"That coot can stay away as long as he likes."

"I don't see why you detest him," Kittie snapped.

"He's so cocksure," I chuckled. "Though the last time I saw him he wasn't so certain as before that Ronnie was alive. He shifted for no reason. I was right about that part of the mystery all the time, Kittie."

"It won't do you any good to be right if you're m-m-murdered." Kittie burst into tears and fled, and just then Mullins called up.

"Your description was cock-eyed," he said. "This Ranova is a big hulking guy."

"Then you caught him at the Stevens Hotel?" That was the address I had given Mullins.

"No, he checked out this morning, but we have a full description of him."

"This will be the fellow who turned the pages for Ranova," I said.

"You didn't say anything about him," Mullins reminded me.

"I was a little excited when I called you. Better come up, Mullins. I've a new theory I want to tell you about."

"I'll drop in within half an hour," he promised.

23

MISS LAWTON IS FOUND

I'VE READ LOTS of detective stories, and in most of them the police get pretty shoddy treatment. They're pictured as stupid, rough and clumsy and they're always being shown up by some amateur detective whose real hobby is Egyptian hieroglyphics or Chinese pottery.

Until the Ray business I'd never come into contact with the police and didn't know anything about their methods. I was pretty impatient at their failure to clean up the Ray business in jigtime. I'd met Forman—he was a very bright fellow, and if it hadn't been for his sudden end, I think he might have got to the bottom of what was puzzling us in time to save a life or two. Williams was supposed to be a star Federal operative, but he had accomplished nothing whatever up to this time. Captain Mullins had no genius, but he was no fool. He wasn't stubborn and he could see through a ladder.

Where the police are strong is in numbers. They had hundreds of good men working on every angle of the business they could get hold of, and it was a headquarters plainclothesman who made the next discovery. Ranova's broadcast was responsible.

The following afternoon a detective discovered that a

man named Ramon Ranova had a safety deposit box in
an uptown branch of the National City Bank, and within
an hour the police had broken open the box. It was full
of Treasury Reserve notes.

It was a big box and it was crammed to the brim. They
counted four hundred and fifty thousand dollars. Much of
it was in five hundred and one thousand dollar bills, but
there was one package tied with big rubber bands which
amounted to two hundred thousand dollars, and this package was entirely one hundred dollar bills.

And the last visit that Ramon Ranova had paid to his
deposit box was the day after the kidnaping of Barbara
Bond.

The police decided that the two hundred thousand was
Barbara's ransom money and that the balance was part
of what the blackmailers had taken in cash from Ronald
Ray. It was placed in the bank to be released only on order
from the Police Commissioner, and it clinched my theory
that Ranova was the person who had attempted to murder
Barbara, and undoubtedly also the blackmailer of Ronnie
and the leader of the kidnapers.

It seemed likely that he would have another deposit box
containing the rest of the money forced out of Ronnie,
though it was possible that this had been paid out to his
confederates.

The police were no longer depressed, but were full of
confidence. They had a description of the killer, blackmailer
and kidnaper, and that description was broadcasted. It
wouldn't be long, Mullins assured me, before they'd have
Ranova under the lights and force a full explanation from
him of the things which were still puzzling us.

In a couple of days Barbara would be well enough to revisit Millford and help the officers identify the cottage in which she had been confined. I'd had several long talks with her. She had become thoroughly convinced that Ronnie was dead and was reconciled to her loss.

Meanwhile we had a couple of authors concocting scripts for the perfume mystery program. After her experience of the other morning, Madame Duplon had agreed with Kittie that talking broadcasts were the thing. What finally persuaded her and her husband was the fear lest Locatelli's superstitions get abroad, and people get the notion that Perfumes of Arcady were as unlucky as opals. Kittie put that notion into their heads.

I was reading one of the scripts, which was pretty exciting, when the door opened and in came Kittie, looking thrilled to death and escorting Lita Lawton.

Miss Lawton was dressed exactly as she had been the last time I saw her. She looked thinner, if possible, and her eyes were sort of staring. I jumped up and pumped her hand. I certainly was glad to see her.

"Well, well, well!" I exclaimed. "Where on earth have you been? Don't you know the authorities have been trying to find you for a week or more?"

Miss Lawton opened her bag and dug out her pad of writing paper.

I grinned. "Don't bother," I told her. "Speak right out. We're all friends, here."

She stared at me as if I were crazy and scribbled:

I don't understand. You know my affliction.

I glanced at the note and sniffed. "We've found out you can talk, Miss Lawton," I remarked. "It was a slick act, but it's no longer necessary. Iona Ivar told us you could talk as well as anybody."
She scribbled some more:

> *I had a growth in my throat ten years ago. It was cut out, but my vocal cords have been paralyzed since. I was sorry to hear of Iona's death. I once played accompaniments for her.*

"Oh," exclaimed Kittie remorsefully. "We didn't understand. I'm so sorry, Miss Lawton."
She smiled sort of bitterly and nodded.
She wrote:

> *I didn't want to see the police. They pestered me so. I've been living in a lodging house in Stamford, but so many awful things have happened I felt it my duty to come back and tell what I know. I thought if I told everything to you, they might not bother me. I don't want to see detectives. They frighten me.*

"Well, that's swell," I said.
She wrote:

> *I don't know where to begin. You ask questions.*

"Did you know that Ronnie was being blackmailed?"
She wrote:

> *Yes. But I didn't know by whom. He wouldn't tell me that. Ever since he got in the big money, he has been paying nearly every cent*

he made to somebody.

"But he lived at the Ritz," I pointed out.

> *He was allowed to pay me my ten per cent. I gave him the money for living expenses and to make a show.*

"Why?" I demanded.

> *Because I was making what seemed a fortune to me. I didn't want Ronnie to quit work.*

"Do you know why he was blackmailed?" I asked eagerly. She nodded and wrote:

> *Please give me a large sheet of paper.*

Kittie placed one in front of her instantly.
THE WOMAN DREW her chair up to my desk and began to write at length. We waited with increasing excitement. She wrote fast in a crabbed hand. When the sheet was full I grasped it and Kittie placed another in front of her, so that she wrote without interruption.

> *A little more than two years ago I was living alone in a little house on the outskirts of Syracuse. I had been a pianist in vaudeville and I had played the piano in picture houses. But vaudeville was dead and even the smallest picture house was using sound films and had discharged the house musicians. I had saved a few hundred dollars but the money was almost gone.*
>
> *I didn't know what would become of me.*

Well, one evening there was a knock at my back door and a tramp stood there. He was very thin and unshaven but he was a very handsome young man nevertheless, and even if I'm middle-aged and ugly, I'm a woman and I was impressed.

He asked me for something to eat. I put food in front of him on the kitchen table and he ate voraciously. My heart went out to him. When he had finished, he laid his head on the table and wept like a baby. I stroked his hair. He kissed my hand.

"You're the first person who has been kind to me," he said.

"What is your name?"

I pointed to my mouth, secured a pencil and paper. I wrote, "Lita Lawton. I am dumb on account of an operation on my throat."

"Gosh," he said. "You're in worse luck than I am."

He said he had been sleeping in fields and haystacks for a week and I told him that he could spend the night in my house. I didn't care about my reputation, you see. I only wanted to be kind.

My eyes were full of tears. I passed the sheet of paper to Kittie, who was weeping when Miss Lawton finished. After a minute she had filled a second sheet:

After he had eaten I suggested that he take a bath and put his clothes outside so I could brush and take the spots out of them. He assented joyfully. I took him upstairs to the bathroom and then I went dozen and set up the ironing board and did my best with his zoom, dirty clothes. His linen was filthy—coarse cotton garments. I washed them and hung them up in the kitchen to dry.

I carried up his outer garments and told him to put them on until his underwear was dry. He thanked me so sweetly.

I went downstairs and I felt so happy to be of service to the dear boy that I sat down at my old upright piano for the first time in weeks and began to play.

At first I played Chopin, and then I played ballads with my own transcriptions. I was playing "Suwanee River" when he came into the room and sat dozen quietly.

"That's marvelous," he said.

"Please play it again."

I did and he began to sing. You know his voice. You can imagine how it thrilled me. I became excited. I played another plantation melody, I forget what, and he sang it even more beautifully. I stopped playing, rushed to the desk and wrote.

I wrote, "My dear boy, you have a God-given voice. I have never heard exactly as remarkable a quality. There's a fortune in it."

He read and shook his head.

"Not for me, there isn't," he said.

My hand was shaking as I wrote, I was so excited.

It was the end of the page. I handed it to Kittie, snatched the half page she had written and gave her another sheet of paper.

"I have had lots of experience in music," I wrote. "I know the theater. We'll get a small vaudeville engagement in some picture house and in no time you'll be singing in radio."

The boy buried his face in his hands and sobbed.

"I can't do it," he said. "Miss Lawton, you're awfully good to me. I know you won't betray me.

I can't be seen anywhere. I'm an escaped convict."

"CLARKSON!" I EXCLAIMED. Miss I. Lawton looked up and nodded, and continued writing:

> *He told me his sad story. He was unjustly convicted of burglary in Indianapolis on account of having got into bad company and he had escaped from the state prison. Of course the police everywhere were looking for him.*

The writing ended and I took the next sheet:

> *That seemed to settle my suggestion, but I saw in him my own chance to escape from poverty and I had an inspiration.*
>
> *"You might as well be in prison as tramping around the country, starving and sleeping in fields," I said. "You have to take a chance."*
>
> *"Some cop would recognize me with the footlights beating on me," he replied.*
>
> *"You're going to sing in the dark," I wrote. "It's a marvelous bit of showmanship." And that's why we sang in the dark."*

"But your first appearance when he faced the microphone!" I objected.

She had stopped writing, but took another sheet:

> *It was a mistake. The lights were out when we went on the stage and suddenly went on. I ran out and made them turn them out again. We played several engagements and reached New York and I got Ronnie—Ronald Ray is his real name—Clarkson was a name he took when arrested—an audition at International. Just because we insisted upon singing in the dark it amused them and they gave us our chance. And that's the whole story.*

"It's the most marvelous story I ever heard!" exclaimed Kittie. "Miss Lawton, I think you are wonderful."

"But he couldn't stay in the dark," I remarked. "He went about everywhere. He was photographed."

She scribbled:

> *He had to take those chances. After the first few weeks he felt sure he wouldn't be identified because his appearance was changed by prosperity and it wasn't likely they would connect Ronald Ray the famous singer, with Clarkson the burglar. And the police never did discover him. It was some wretch who had been in prison with him. Ronnie would not tell me who—*

"A small Spanish man named Ramon Ranova?" demanded Kittie excitedly.

She shook her head and wrote:

> *I never saw him. Ronnie met him secretly.*

"Why should anybody want to kill him?" I asked.

She wrung her hands and shook her head.

"Do you know that there is somebody who looks like Ronnie who is one of a gang which kidnaped Miss Bond?"

> *I read that in the papers.*

"This Ramon Ranova has a voice exactly like Ronnie's," cried Kittie, and she told about the broadcast. Miss Lawton wrote:

> *It seems very queer. I suppose no mail has come for me.*

I then explained about the letter and the phonograph record and confessed that the police had it. She wrote:

I don't understand at all. Will you do me a great favor?

"Anything I can," I said heartily.

I am afraid I am guilty of a crime for shielding an escaped convict. I've lost Ronnie. Haven't I suffered enough?

"Oh, I don't think they will prosecute you," I said. "I've found the police are regular guys."

I'm afraid. I've told you all I know. I want to get away now. I'm sure they'll put me in prison.

"Get in a notary," I said to Kittie. "We'll have her swear to what she has written. That ought to satisfy the police, because this is exactly what they wanted to get from her. And after that, Miss Lawton, you can leave the office. They're looking for you, of course, but I'm not going to turn you in."

She smiled, and wrote:

You're very kind. After all, Ronnie and I have reason to be grateful to you.

Kittie looked dubious. "You might get into trouble, Pete," she objected.

"I'll take a chance. This lady has been through enough."

So that's what we did. We had her sign in front of a

notary and take the oath and then we shook hands. I escorted her down to the street myself and wished her good luck after putting her into a cab.

After that I took the statement and went down to see the police commissioner. He called me a lot of vile names for letting her go, blustered, threatened to jail me, and then read the statement, into which Kittie had written my questions.

When the old boy got through he was in a different mood. Miss Lawton's story got him, as it had us.

"This is marvelous," he said. "It certainly tells us a lot that was puzzling. So Ray was Clarkson, not the double. Probably he only knew a couple of songs before the Lawton woman began to teach him. In jail, he didn't feel like singing. Well, Hunter, you had no business letting her go, but after reading this I would have done the same thing. The poor old creature is afraid of being jailed for helping him."

"It's a pathetic story, all right," I said. "Imagine the boy turning over everything he made and his accompanist supporting him."

He nodded. "We're nearing the end. I ought to lock you up, but I'll just shake hands."

We were nearing the end, all right; but it was an entirely different end from the commissioner and I supposed.

24

PRIME HOOTCH

ACCOMPANIED BY STATE officers, Barbara and I drove to Millford two days after the astonishing reappearance of Miss Lawton. Barbara was cured of her cold and was her usual energetic self. She said that what she had needed was food rather than medical attention. I had told her the tale written out and sworn to by Miss Lawton, but apparently it hadn't affected her much. The first night as a prisoner in the hut seemed to have ended her infatuation for Ronnie. She had decided then that the poor chap had been dead for weeks and she had been the victim of a personally humiliating hocus-pocus.

"How awful," she said to me. "If I had married a burglar and an escaped convict. How dared he engage himself to me with a cloud like that hanging over him?"

"You're about the prettiest girl there is," I replied. "The boy fell head over heels in love with you. He wanted you so much he forgot everything. I can understand that."

"But it was so unfair to me," she complained.

I didn't say any more. Barbara was a most contradictory girl. She had gone after Ronnie like a hawk goes after a pigeon. She had proposed to him—she had admitted that to me—and now she was offended because he had lost his head and accepted her.

I would have considered her attitude pretty selfish if I hadn't seen the way she had dashed headlong to his rescue, risking her life twice on a long chance that he wasn't dead but a captive. That certainly was generosity of a very big sort.

Anyway, she seemed to like me a lot and I sunned myself in her smile. Barbara, who had lots of friends, seemed to have dropped them for me. She had refused to see anybody but white-haired Peter Hunter during her illness, and that indicated something.

When we arrived at Millford we were taken to inspect three houses that the authorities had under suspicion. The interior of the first was unfamiliar to her, but when we entered the second one she grasped my arm.

"I feel that this is it," she said. "My room ought to be there."

She pointed to a door off the living room. We went in and Barbara cried out excitedly: "This is it! That's the awful cot I lay on."

"We thought it was," said the local chief of police. "Is this one of your hair-pins, Miss Bond?"

He extended her a yellow hair-pin.

She nodded.

The chief grinned. "Solid gold," he said. "We were pretty sure, but wanted you to identify the place positively. We found evidence of recent occupation. Found a big yellow dog about a hundred yards away that had been poisoned. A lot of cans, out back, recently opened. They weren't rusty."

"Any clues to the occupants?" I demanded.

"Not a thing. Tire tracks in the dirt driveway but of a very common tread. That was no help."

"Well," said Barbara, "the place gives me the creeps. I want to go home."

"Okay," said the state officer in charge. "This place is just six miles out of Millford, Miss Bond. There's a lake at the foot of these woods and you were lucky you didn't fall into it in the dark. The house belongs to a carpenter in Millford who rents it out. The crooks just took possession of it."

"Come and have dinner with me tonight," said Barbara when we started back for New York.

"Gosh I'd like to, but I have a dinner engagement with Kittie. Why not the three of us?" I suggested.

"No," she said pettishly. "I don't feel like a threesome."

"But Kittie is awfully fond of you. She was saying this morning she was anxious to see you."

"I like her, too," she replied. "But I'm tired. I haven't my strength back. I think I'd rather stay home and dine alone. Ask her to come to my house for tea, tomorrow afternoon at five."

"I know she'll love it. I could dine with you tomorrow night."

"We'll see how I feel tomorrow."

I left her at her house and, as it was five o'clock, I went directly to the apartment. Officer Watts was on duty. He was sitting in the living room looking very fondly at a pinch bottle of Scotch—the finest brand there is.

"I couldn't have resisted very much longer," he said with a grin. "How about opening this up, Pete?"

"An inspiration. Where did we get it? I haven't any 'Grand McNish,'" I said.

"Came about ten minutes ago. Compliments of the commissioner," Watts explained.

"There is a swell guy," I exclaimed.

Watts nodded agreement. "I'll get ice and soda," he said. "This stuff costs six bucks a bottle and it's a fifth, at that."

As I pulled the cork, the bell rang and I opened up. In walked Wooster Williams.

"You've a keen scent," I said. "Hey, Watts, get a glass for the Department of Justice."

"I won't say no," remarked Williams. "I've a bone to pick with you, but I'll have a drink first. Why in hell did you let that woman get away?"

"I got a sworn statement out of her."

"Yes. I've seen that, but I have to have a talk with her. You knew she was wanted at police headquarters. You had no damn business—"

"NOW LOOK HERE!" I said belligerently. "I'm not a member of the police department. She told us all she knew and I didn't see why the poor old thing should be given third-degree methods. She oughtn't to be hard to find. Go find her yourself."

Officer Watts set down three glasses and I poured three drinks. The officer put in the charged water and lifted his glass.

"Here's to the commissioner," he toasted.

"Why?" asked Williams.

"He sent Hunter the bottle. Best brand of Scotch there is."

"What's that? Don't touch those drinks!" shouted Williams. "Lay them down!"

The expression on the policeman's face was pitiful.

"I'll call the commissioner," he said grabbing the telephone. Headquarters reported that the commissioner had left an hour before. Williams called the residence and got his man.

"Wooster Williams, speaking. Did you send Peter Hunter a bottle of Scotch? No? Then send a chemist up here to analyze it, please," said Williams sharply.

I turned pale and dropped into a chair. Watt's mouth was opening and shutting like a fish out of the water.

The G-man I'd called a sophomore grinned at me exasperatingly.

"No brains," he said. "You let that woman walk out of your office twice. You have shadows and bodyguards because of three attempts on your life, and you start to guzzle a bottle of whisky that somebody sticks through your front door. I bet you ten dollars to a quarter it's poisoned."

"I—I won't take the bet," I muttered. "The cork came out kind of easy."

"I saved the lives of two asses," he said objectionably. "If I had been one minute later—"

"Maybe it isn't poisoned," muttered Officer Watts, who was blue-green.

Williams took out the cork, smelled of it and sniffed at the bottle.

"I think I detect a faint trace of arsenic. Or perhaps aconite—"

For Watts went down with a crash. He had fainted. The Federal man chuckled heartlessly.

"The battle is still on, it appears," he said. "Let him alone.

He'll come to in a minute. I don't suppose you've doped out why they're after your scalp?"

"No, but I've turned up about everything that has been learned about the Ray case. You and the police have a perfect score—zero," I came back.

"This Ranova is an interesting development," he said. "Hello, Watts. How's tricks?"

The cop was sitting up. I helped him to a couch and he pulled out a red bandanna and wiped his forehead.

"I'm on the wagon from now on," he declared. "All liquor is poison. That's what my old woman says."

"WE NOW KNOW that Ranova, not Ray's double, has the singing voice," said Williams ignoring the unhappy policeman. "Which proves that you experts were mistaken in identifying Ranova's voice as Ray's. And, of course it removes all doubt that it was Ray's body you discovered in Jersey."

He answered the doorbell and admitted a police chemist who sniffed at the bottle but made no comment.

"Arsenic?" asked Williams.

"Wouldn't want to say. I'll phone you the result of the test in an hour."

"You got more lives than a cat," remarked Watts to me. "I'll go down and see the priest and take the pledge as soon as I get off duty."

"Much obliged, Williams," I said after a minute. "I thought maybe the information I'd given had resulted in something important, so I didn't doubt that the commissioner sent the stuff up."

"Why are these attempts at assassination kept up?" Williams demanded. "There is no question that part of the money in the Ranova deposit box is Miss Bond's ransom. She escaped and is safe in her home, well guarded. That stupid, purposeless broadcast of Ranova's cost them a vast sum of money—because otherwise the police wouldn't have discovered Ranova's safety deposit box.

"It revealed that the Ray voice which made the phonograph record and sang 'Barbara Allen' over the phone to Miss Bond belongs to Ranova, and ended their chance to get more money from Miss Bond. They're washed up and don't seem to know it."

"Loots like they're fighting for their lives, now," said Watts surprisingly, "and Hunter's the boy they have to dispose of."

"I don't know who they are," I said sullenly. "I haven't got a thing on them, the fools."

"Will you let me bring in a hypnotist?" asked Williams eagerly.

"No!" I shouted.

"Your subconscious mind—"

"I think I'm going to get angry with you in another minute, Williams," I said.

He laughed. "Okay. Now, don't eat any candy that parties unknown send you, and make sure your police shadows are on the job when you go out."

"You've been down South. What did you find out?" I asked to change the subject.

"Several very interesting things. I consider my trip was profitable."

"Well, what are they?"

"If you don't mind I won't discuss them until I have a chance to check up with certain things here in New York."

"You want me to tell you everything and you tell me nothing. Find relatives of poor Iona Ivar on your travels South?"

He nodded. "A sister in very poor circumstances in Richmond."

"What did she say?"

He grinned in his exasperating manner. "I said I couldn't discuss it. I'm on my way."

"Kittie is dining with me tonight, and how do you like that?"

He hesitated at the door. "Oh? Mind if I join you?"

"I certainly do. Two's company and three's a crowd."

"Then I'll go up and call on Miss Bond." He was good at a comeback.

"Try and get in. She says she wants to be alone tonight."

"Then I'm out of luck," he admitted.

He wasn't, though, as I found out later. Barbara admitted him and invited him to stay to dinner. He was a guy I didn't think had any sex appeal, but women seemed to think differently.

25

THE SHOOTING AT THE ENNIS HOTEL

THE CHEMIST'S REPORT on the whisky was that it contained enough arsenic to kill a troop of horses, and I was in bad shape when I called for Kittie to take her to dinner. Naturally I had to tell her what had happened, and to admit it when she triumphantly demanded whether it hadn't made me change my mind about Wooster Williams.

"He thinks quick, all right," I said. "Though if I'd had any sense I should have been suspicious of gift liquor. No doubt he's all right at trailing bank robbers and gangsters, but he has a crazy streak in him. Trying to get me to consent to being hypnotized! How can I be a menace to criminals I never encountered?"

"It's either that, or somebody hates you horribly," Kittie remarked.

"I never did anything to anybody. I don't believe anybody hates me."

"I do, sometimes," she said with an impish grin. "When you get so opinionated and insist on doing foolish things."

"Well, aside from you, nobody hates me; and almost nobody goes round trying to kill a person even if they do hate him."

"It has something to do with the attempt to prevent a successor to Ronald Ray," she said, knitting her white forehead. "That's why Iona was murdered and why Madame Duplon was notified to listen in on the Ranova broadcast. You're the man who hired Ronnie, and who will hire his successor. Maybe that's why they want to kill you."

"But Duplon would simply hire another advertising agent. It's perfectly preposterous! Ranova, of course, is some nut. Because he has a voice like Ronnie's he thought Madame Duplon would hire him if she heard him over the radio station."

"But you think he's the man that Barbara choked when he was going to stab her in that awful place at Millford— the one who sang 'Barbara Allen'."

"Well, it looks like it," I answered.

"But since Ronnie was killed before he learned the song—if it was something that only the two of them knew about—how did this perfectly unknown Spaniard know that the song meant anything to Barbara?"

"Please, Kittie, let's go eat and take in a show and not talk about this business any more. I can't stand it, honest."

She looked contrite. "I don't blame you. Only it's hard to put it out of my mind."

"Let's dine at the Waldorf and take in a musical."

"That will be nice," she stated.

We had a good dinner with wine, and we saw a rip-snorting musical comedy and then we went dancing. It was two o'clock when I arrived at my apartment. When I let myself in I found the living room brightly lighted and three men sitting at a card table playing "blackjack."

One was Captain Mullins, one was Wooster Williams and the third was the night-shift police bodyguard.

"Make yourselves right at home," I said. "For God's sake what has happened?"

"Miss Bond has been badly wounded," said Williams gravely.

"How? Where? When? For Heaven's sake—"

"By a bullet," said Williams gravely. "In the Ennis Hotel on Broadway at Ninetieth Street, in Room 456, by a blond woman registered as Helen Harvey."

"What does she say?"

"She's in a coma at the Mercy Hospital. They think she will live, but she was wounded in the left side dangerously near the heart."

The shock was almost too much. I got dizzy and I had to be helped to a chair.

"Did you catch the murderer?" I cried hysterically. "What are you fools doing here? Get busy!"

"We're doing everything we can do. We want to talk to you," said Captain Mullins. "It was attempted murder, not murder."

"Talk, talk, that's all you do while killers and poisoners are running amuck," I yelled.

Williams laid a hand on my shoulder.

"Snap out of it," he said sternly. "We know you're in love with Miss Bond. We make allowances for the shock you've had. But you've been closer to her than anybody, Hunter. You might know—"

"I don't know anything! I don't know anything about anything!" I groaned.

"I went up to call on her," said Williams, sitting down

beside me. "She was very gracious. I dined with her and left shortly after nine o'clock. The butler says that she received a letter by special messenger about ten-thirty and immediately ordered her car and drove directly to the Ennis Hotel. The plainclothesman on duty outside her house followed her in a taxi, but she lost him in traffic."

"That woman violates every traffic rule there is," growled Mullins.

"HE DIDN'T GET far behind," said I Williams. "She ran through a signal light at Eighty-sixth street and Broadway. He was blocked by other cars and his taxi couldn't follow. However, he spotted her car parked directly in front of a hydrant outside the Ennis Hotel. It was empty. He inquired inside and she had taken an elevator to the fourth floor. There are fifty rooms on each floor, so he thought he had better wait in the lobby until she came down. She hadn't had herself announced, so he couldn't find out which room she was visiting."

"A few minutes later somebody phoned down from the fourth floor that a revolver shot had been fired in a room close by. It was the occupant of room 454 who telephoned. The house dick, who had been talking with Murphy, the headquarters man, was notified. He and Murphy went up in the elevator. There were people in the corridor outside the door of room 456, and the man who had phoned down said he was sure that was the room.

"The door was locked and they broke it open and found Miss Bond lying unconscious and bleeding from a wound in her side. The would-be murderer had escaped."

"As usual," I said bitterly.

He shrugged. "They got a description, of course. A

plump blonde about thirty-five or forty. She had rented the room without baggage and paid in advance for it. She told the clerk that her trunk would arrive the next day. Do you know of any acquaintance of Miss Bond who answers that description?"

"I never met any of her friends and acquaintances," I said. "Kittie might know. She and Barbara were quite thick for a couple of weeks after Ronnie disappeared."

"The letter which lured her there was not on her person," Williams explained. "It looks as though the gun-woman had removed it, knowing it would be a valuable clue. You're in her confidence. Can you think of any reason why Miss Bond would rush out to a second-rate hotel at that hour on receipt of a message?"

I shook my head.

"She told me at dinner that she was convinced that Ray was dead," Williams said. "And that no matter how persuasive the scoundrels might be, nothing would induce her to pay any further attention to their phone calls or messages."

"Maybe this woman had something on her," said the materialistic police captain. "This Bond girl has run pretty wild you know. Suppose she threatened an exposure?"

"Take him away before I have to hit him," I implored Williams.

"I believe that the attempt to kill Miss Bond—this is the second attempt on her life—the third, come to think of it—I think it has the same motive which caused the attempts on your life, Hunter. You and she are in it together. Does that give you an idea?"

I shook my head. Lord, how dense I was!

"Come on, Captain," said Williams. "She's going to live, old man," he assured me. "Don't worry too much. Try to get some sleep."

"Where are we going?" demanded Mullins.

"There is a possibility that the girl didn't take the letter with her," Williams replied.

"It's a cinch she would. Women always do things like that."

"Nevertheless we'd better go right up to her place and search her desk. We've been here an hour and a half, Hunter. Why the devil don't you keep decent hours?"

I knew how to touch him. "Kittie and I went dancing," I said.

He scowled. "How many women do you want?" he asked in a surly tone. "Come on, Mullins."

I took a stiff drink after they left and turned in, but of course I couldn't sleep. Thinking of Barbara; that beautiful, brave girl, with a bullet in her side, fighting for her life. How could anybody sleep?

I got up after an hour, called the hospital and was handed the old hooey, "Resting comfortably." I was tempted to call Kittie, but why spoil the child's night rest. She'd hear about this awful thing soon enough.

After that I played blackjack with the cop, who had slept all day, couldn't sleep on duty, and was glad of my company.

26

THE PRESS BOOK

THE NEXT MORNING I arrived at the office at quarter of nine, to the astonishment of the staff. Even Kittie wasn't at her desk at that hour. In about a quarter of an hour, however, a special messenger brought me a note from my secretary. I'd been ripping things up looking for a contract I was supposed to sign. Kittie could lay her hands on it in a moment. The note meant she was sick or something.

I tore open the letter and this is what it said. We were always formal in communications:

> Dear Mr. Hunter:
> At eight this morning, Miss Lawton called me on the phone. She's ill and alone and thinks she's going to die and has something very important to tell me. I'm going to see her and probably won't be in until twelve or one o'clock, as I have to go out of town. She's terrified of the police, poor soul, and I promised not to say where she is staying.
>
> Kittie Ketchum.

It was annoying to have Kittie out of the office, but she had done the right thing, of course, in answering the summons. It was a mystery to me how that dumb old maid could continue to avoid the army of cops on the lookout for her, but maybe she'd tell Kittie something that would shed a little more light on the mystery.

I went outside and asked a couple of clerks to find the contract and I went through Kittie's desk myself. Come to think of it, the contract had been laying on my desk yesterday, but it certainly wasn't there now.

There is a closet in my private office where things get put that don't go into a filing cabinet—the things which lie around on top of tables and bookshelves in every office. Kittie usually goes into it as a last resort and often finds what she wants. I tackled it and there was the contract on a shelf in front of my eyes, lying on top of a black scrap book and a pile of magazines. I picked it up and glanced at the scrap book, which I vaguely remembered.

"Good Lord!" I exclaimed. Iona Ivar had had it under her arm the day she came in. She had laid it down and hadn't said anything about it, and I'd never given it a thought. Of course, my mind wasn't functioning any too well that day, on account of a lot of things.

The police had been asking for information about Iona, but by that time I'd completely forgotten the book. The cleaning woman had got tired of looking at it and stuck it in the closet.

Williams had gone South on the back-trail of the murdered woman. All he'd discovered was that she had a sister in Richmond. He'd raise hell if he knew I had this record of her pitiful career.

I took the book of press clippings to my desk. Maybe it would enable me to tell Williams something he didn't know.

I had no other motive for looking at that book than a silly antagonism to Williams. Even if he had saved my life the day before, he irritated me. There was a lot of important work for me to do and I let it wait. I sat down and opened the scrap book the achievements of an unfortunate woman who had been cut off when she was on the point of amounting to something for the first time in her life.

On the first page was the program of a vaudeville house in Birmingham, Alabama. It was dated 1907—nearly thirty years ago. That made Iona pretty near fifty years old. Well, she had pretty near looked it.

Old theater programs have always fascinated me. On this bill were a couple of headliners I remembered as a kid—Jim and Bonnie Thornton.

It opened with a dog act and in second spot was Iona Ivar; "sweet singer," according to the billing.

I turned the page. A New Orleans house, 1908. Poor Iona had opened the show. There followed the garish, cheaply-colored programs of honky-tonks in St. Louis and Nashville. The best spot she had in these was third place, and there were stretches of weeks and months between engagements. There followed Chatauqua programs in small Southern towns, yellowed newspaper clippings reviewing the bills and placing Iona among the also-rans. I saw no mention of her accompanist. She must have taken pot-luck at that period.

There came a bill at a vaudeville house in Atlanta in 1912. Iona was in the second spot on that bill (nobody can possibly go well in second spot) but for the first time she was billed as a Female Baritone. As I was about to turn the page I caught another name and I stiffened with attention.

Alice Warren, Woman Protean.

Protean... Protean, what did that mean? Funny way to
describe a pianist... Absently I turned the pages. 1914,
1917—infrequent engagements always for Iona. In 1920,
there was another string of Chautauqua programs—apparently the same troupe traveled all over the South. And Iona
Ivar, female baritone, was the headliner. And at the bottom
of the program, in small type:

Alice Warren at the piano.

Protean... I remembered what it meant. I remembered
seeing, fifteen years ago, the great Protean artist Jacques
Duval. Pantomimist and Protean. Sure—a grandiloquent
vaudeville name for a performer who did an entire playlet
and played all characters, male and female, by swift changes
of costume and appearance.

I turned back to the old bill in Atlanta.

Alice Warren, Protean.

And all of a sudden it meant something to me. Why,
the Lawton woman had been an actress—one who played
many parts—who could completely change her appearance!

I SLAMMED THE scrapbook shut. This was something!
Why, it explained a lot. It explained why she had disappeared twice without the police being able to find her. A
few changes in her appearance and she could pass right
under the noses of the thick-headed flatfeet.

She was clever, all right. I'd admitted that. Hadn't she

devised the Singer in the Dark, which had put Ronald Ray over? Apparently she had failed to make the big-time with her act, and eventually couldn't get bookings any more, which explained why she was playing the piano at Chautauquas.

Excitedly I started at the back of the book, where the most recent stuff was pasted, and went through the mass of steadily dwindling and less important engagements. But Alice Warren's name didn't appear again. The book was just the record of the pitiful career of a dead woman.

I reached for the telephone—and pulled back my hand. The police would get excited if they learned that Lita Lawton was a quick-change artist. They would jump to conclusions and make things hard for her. Since she had told everything she knew to Kittie and myself and had sworn to her statement before a notary, what difference did it make how she avoided capture? What of it, if twenty years before, when she could talk, she had been a character actress?

I drummed on my desk. Williams had a right to know this. I asked the operator to call him, and he answered almost immediately.

"Hello, Hunter. Just had a flash from the hospital. Miss Bond will pull through, but she's still unconscious."

"Can you come down here?" I asked. "I've got some fresh dope on Iona Ivar."

"I'm practically there," he assured me. He didn't exaggerate much. In ten minutes he walked into the office. Jaunty as usual.

"Williams," I said, "the day Iona Ivar called here, I was under a mental strain. When she came in she laid down a scrapbook on the table there and said something about her press notices. I didn't pay any attention. My idea was to get her out as soon as possible, but when she brought in the name of Lita Lawton I got interested and the information she gave me about her caused me to completely forget the press book.

"I'll be hanged!" exclaimed Williams. "I told you I was going South to try to get a line on her, and you had her press book in your office all the time!"

"Well, I found it—by accident," I said with a grin. "I've gone through it. Wooster, you really went South to see what more you could find about Lita Lawton, didn't you?"

"Yes. That was the only reason I was interested in Ivar. She knew her years ago. I might find others who could tell me about the Lawton woman."

"I can tell you," I said complacently. "Twenty years ago she wasn't playing the piano. She was in vaudeville, doing a Protean act."

"I never could afford to go to college," Williams said with embarrassment. "What on earth is that?"

"Well, I didn't know myself, at first; but I remembered. It's a term for an actor who plays all the characters in a show by quick changes of costume. He talks in half a dozen voices—"

Williams' eyes were shining. He thumped my desk with clenched fist. "I knew you had the clue!" he exclaimed. "It's about time you produced it!"

"I only found this out five minutes ago. Iona Ivar left the book here after an attempt had been made on my life—"

"Never mind. Go on!"

"Doesn't this explain how Lita Lawton keeps out of the hands of the police?"

"It does," he said grimly. "It explains a lot more than that. Hunter, you ought to be jailed for not holding that woman on both occasions when you had her in your hands."

"Is that so!"

"LET ME TELL you something," continued the Federal man. "I didn't find out about this quick-change business, but I found out something else from the sister of Iona Ivar. In 1923, Iona and Alice Warren did a sister act on the Texas five-a-day circuit. *Two* female baritones, Mr. Hunter."

I gaped at him.

"Iona forgot to mention that," he said smiling, "when she told you about Alice Warren having been her pianist. She had what she thought were her reasons, no doubt. I went over that sworn statement of Lawton's," Williams went on. "It contains several inaccuracies. Her explanation of the 'Singing in the Dark' business, for instance."

"What!" I interrupted.

"Ray sang in the dark because he couldn't sing a note," Williams declared "Lita Lawton did the singing. Iona Ivar knew it."

"Indeed? Then why didn't she tell me?"

"Ivar knew that Lawton had vanished. She was afraid, if you found out that the Ronald Ray voice wasn't dead, you'd persuade Lita Lawton to come out of hiding and take the perfume program. Ivar wanted that job."

"If she knew the thing was a fake, which I can't believe, why didn't she expose Lawton?" I argued.

"One trouper doesn't expose another. Don't you see why

Lawton faked dumbness? If the pianist was known to be
a dummy, no suspicion would attach to the 'singing in the
dark' business."

"She did say that Miss Lawton wasn't dumb," I admitted.

"Iona Ivar knew altogether too much," continued
Wooster Williams. "Which is why she died."

I must have turned pale. "Do you mean she stabbed
Miss Ivar?"

"I do. And tried to kill Barbara Bond in the house at
Millford."

"But that was a man!" I protested.

"Protean artist," he explained. "Miss Bond described her
antagonist as a small man. Although armed, Miss Bond
overpowered her. It's very seldom that a woman can get
the better of a man in a fight."

"You mean to say you've built up this horrible theory on
what I've just told you?" I asked.

"Partly. I believe, now, that Ranova was Lita Lawton.
She knew the significance of the song 'Barbara Allen.' And
it's certain Lawton was the voice of Ronald Ray. Don't you
see that nobody else could know that Ray was going to
learn 'Barbara Allen' to sing to his fiancée? Of course he
had to tell his accompanist, since she was the singer. That
explains why the kidnapers knew about the song."

"Yes, but a lot of things don't jibe," I objected. "You're
taking a lot for granted."

"After we left you last night," Williams said gravely, "I
went up to Miss Bond's house with Mullins and we went
through her desk. We found the note which lured her to
the Ennis Hotel. The police have it, but this is about what
it said:

Dear Miss Bond:

There are some things about Ronnie I would like to tell you.
Things which you will want to know. As the police are searching
for me and I'm horribly afraid of them, I cannot call on you, but I
am in room 456 in the Ennis Hotel on Broadway at Ninetieth. I
am leaving New York forever in the morning. Do not announce
yourself, but come directly to my room. I shall be waiting for you
until one o'clock.

Lita Lawton.

I swallowed hard. "But the assassin was a plump, blond woman," I objected.

"Protean artist," he retorted. "Lita Lawton assumed Miss Bond would bring the note with her. That was her error. She opened the door and said she would call Miss Lawton. Barbara entered and the woman shot at her. She fled instantly—probably escaped by the stairs and the Ladies' entrance. Perhaps she was already some other personality when Barbara entered, so she could go down in the elevator without being recognized as the woman in Room 456."

"All right," I said slowly. "Assuming that this old maid is a fiend, for the sake of argument, I can see a motive for killing Iona Ivar, who was in a position to expose her. But what could she have against Barbara Bond? And do you credit her with the attempt to murder me? She had nothing against me, certainly."

"I appreciate that. Frankly, I always had a feeling that Lawton was very much mixed up in this. When I learned that she hadn't been dumb ten years ago, it flashed on me that maybe she was the Singer in the Dark and Ray was just the front. When I came back, I was flabbergasted to find out that a man named Ranova owned the Ray voice. I was puzzled at her motive when I found her letter to Miss Bond last night because it was fairly obvious that Ranova had sung 'Barbara Allen' through the wall in the cottage in Millford, and afterwards attacked Miss Bond with a knife. I admit I can't understand why she has it in for you and Miss Bond."

"You're mad," I muttered.

He stared at me. "And you're damn near crazy. What's the matter with you?" he demanded.

With a trembling hand I passed over to him the note I had received from Kittie.

He read it—and the cocky, snappy self confident detective grew white as a ghost.

"The same writing, almost the same message Lita Lawton sent Miss Bond," he mumbled.

"You mean she's sent for Kittie to murder her? I gasped.

But Williams had snatched his hat and was rushing out of the office.

27

KITTIE KETCHUM ON THE SPOT

I WAS SO weak I could hardly lift myself from my chair, but I staggered after him. When I reached the hall he had stepped into an elevator the door of which slammed.

I had to help myself along by the wall. My knees were hardly able to support my body. My employees gazed at me with concern as I crossed the outer office.

"Are you ill, Mr. Hunter?" asked the phone operator anxiously.

"I—I'm all right," I muttered and gained my sanctum. I collapsed into my chair.

Not Kittie… Surely the fiend wouldn't murder Kittie. My Kittie! The finest, straightest, sweetest, bravest little woman in the world.

I was perspiring cold sweat from every pore. I was absolutely in anguish. I'd never felt like this, not even when they carried off Barbara Bond or when it seemed that Barbara was dying in the hospital. Why, I couldn't get along without Kittie. I couldn't live without her. Kittie and I had gone side by side through adversity and prosperity. She was part of me.

Damn it, I was in love with her. I'd been in love with her for years! And that's why I couldn't tolerate Williams.

He was in love with her and she with him, by the looks of things.

I called Kittie's apartment. Maybe she hadn't gone. Maybe she hadn't found the place and had returned. But there was no answer to her telephone. I hung up and stared at the wall. Kittie had been kind to Lita Lawton. Surely the woman could have no animosity against Kittie. If she hated Barbara, it was because Barbara was engaged to Ronnie.

I had to believe Williams's theory. The letter the woman had sent to Barbara confirmed it. And, just the way a flash of lightning splits a black cloud, I understood what he couldn't understand—the motive. What a fool I had been! Williams had insisted that the explanation of the whole mystery was in my office—that, in my subconscious mind. It was. I knew the why of everything. And it was as plain as the nose on my face.

Lita Lawton was wildly in love with Ronnie Ray. She had guarded and guided him to success. He leaned on her for everything. Hers was the golden voice; Ronnie, the handsome, front. And suddenly he became infatuated with Barbara Bond; broke with Lita, defied her.

The day after the engagement he had vanished. Lita had killed him, executed him. But no! How could she, a woman, arrange that awful death for him?

Assume she had done it somehow. She hated Barbara as a jilted woman hates her rival. She hated me because I was responsible for bringing them together. That's why my life had been attempted, why she double-crossed her confederates, who wanted money from Barbara, and had attempted to knife her. Of course the man with the knife was this Protean artist. Williams was right. And she must hate Kittie, just because Kittie was associated with me. Kittie might be a corpse already.

If Williams rescued Kittie, it would bring them together. She would marry him, maybe, and break my heart. I didn't know what to do, where to turn. Of course Lita Lawton was mad, a homicidal maniac.

I was walking the floor. It was all a nightmare. That little, wizened, dumb murderess! But I could see a reason, now, for everything.

In a burst of insane fury she killed her lover. In the statement of hers which had moved Kittie and me so, she said she had washed his linen and cleaned his clothes the night he came to her door. She had been infatuated with him then. And his was a personality to match the amazing voice in her plain little body. And she had a grip on him because he was an escaped convict.

After the crime, she had regretted it. Judging by the money in the safety deposit box she had been making him turn over to her all his earnings, and the golden flood had stopped. During the weeks succeeding his death she had hated Barbara and me—and Kittie—more and more, considering us responsible for her horrible act.

Being a performer, she suffered from the loss of her employment. And then she had found a double for Ronald Ray and it occurred to her that she might pass him off as Ronnie and get back on the Perfume hour if Barbara and I—and Kittie, who knew Ronnie best—were out of the way.

However, she didn't have things all her own way any more. Her confederates, who had helped murder Ray, wanted to get ransom from Barbara. By accident Kittie and I had discovered Ronnie's body. The woman set out to persuade the world that it wasn't Ray's body, that he could be ransomed and go on "Singing in the Dark," as before.

Hence the renewed attempt to get ransom money and possession of Barbara Bond. That was why she had her mail forwarded to my office; so she could send the phonograph record which seemed to prove Ray was alive.

Barbara's escape balked her scheme. She then conceived the notion of dispensing with the double, assuming the personality of Ramon Ranova, and inducing Madame Duplon, through the broadcast at International, to engage Ranova because his voice was exactly like Ronnie Ray's.

Oh, I had worked it all out; but what was the use if she murdered Kittie Ketchum? And I'd never had a chance to tell Kittie I loved her.... Not that it would have done any good. I'd made a fool of myself with Barbara Bond.

TWO HOURS WENT by while I was crazy like that. Clients were announced and I refused to see them. My mind was galloping like a race horse, but to no purpose. I'd have tackled ten men with my naked hands to save Kittie, and I didn't know how to start looking for her.

My phone was ringing and I ignored it. Finally the operator, with a frightened face—I had barked at her on a previous appearance—opened my door.

"Miss Ketchum is on the line," she said.

With a spring like a tiger I was upon the phone.

"Kittie!" I cried. "For God's sake, are you all right?"

"Yes, I'm all right," said Kittie, rather surprised, I thought. "I'm with Miss Lawton."

"Where? Kittie, I've suffered anguish!"

"Really? I wrote you a note."

"You treacherous rat!" she snarled, and pulled the trigger

"I have it! That's why—"

"Miss Lawton is much better," Kittie said. "I've the most amazing news—"

"Where are you?" I almost screamed.

"She came in with me. We'll be at my apartment. I'd like you to come up here now if you can." Kittie hung up before I could answer. I immediately called back and the operator at her apartment house reported that her phone didn't answer.

"But she's just hung up. I talked with her," I protested.

"I'm sorry, but Miss Ketchum's phone has not been in use," reported the operator.

I sat there stupefied. Where was Williams? The last place he'd look for Kittie was at her apartment. Only she wasn't at her apartment. She hadn't told the truth. Why should Kittie lie?

She hadn't sounded as though she were frightened. Her voice was perfectly natural. Knowing Kittie's loyalty I didn't

think that torture could force her to lure me into a trap.
And, by the way she talked, she was on the best of terms
with the Lawton woman. Of course she didn't know what
I knew about the creature. She hadn't seen the note which
had induced Barbara to walk into a hotel room to be shot
down.

Was it all a mare's nest? Was somebody making use
of Lawton's name—the same person who had forged
Ronnie's handwriting in the note which had accompanied
the phonograph record? No, the woman was a homicidal
maniac. Everything fitted perfectly. And, without being
aware of it, Kittie was bait for a trap. A trap for me.

Should I call Captain Mullins and go up there with a
squad of police? Burst in, assuming they were at Kittie's
apartment? I didn't dare. An ordinary criminal might hesitate to kill with the police at the door, but if my theories
were correct, this woman was insane. She wouldn't hesitate
to slay Kittie.

I had my gun permit and on my hip was a new automatic
pistol. I had to go up there alone. I had one advantage. The
woman had no notion that I suspected her of a list of horrible crimes. She might have some purpose other than my
immediate death and I'd shoot her like a dog to save Kittie.

I called Williams on the offchance that he was at his
apartment, but there was no answer.

"Don't know when I'll be back," I told the phone operator as I left the Hunter Agency. There was a good chance
I might never return.

I hailed a cab and gave Kittie's address. She lived in
a smart apartment house on Fifty-eighth Street, near
Madison Avenue. During the trip uptown through traffic

I suffered plenty, but not once did I think of funking the visit nor of calling in the police to help me. If anything happened to Kittie, I didn't give a darn what happened to me.

A mind skips about under stress. I thought of Barbara Bond, recovering from her wound in the hospital. I had been dazed by the girl's amazing beauty, but I had never been in love with her. Just flattered by the friendship of an enormously rich young woman. That night we had driven up to Bear Mountain I had been so frightened I almost hated her. It would take a better man than Peter Hunter to control that extraordinary girl. While I wasn't the type who can be dominated by a wife—well, I guessed Kittie could do as she pleased with me. She had pretty near bossed the Hunter Agency. She'd saved me from a thousand blunders with her sharp tongue and solid good sense.

28

THE MAD KILLER

THE CAB DREW up before the apartment building. I paid off the taxi driver and entered. The telephone operator, who knew me very well, nodded and smiled.

"Is Miss Ketchum at home, do you know?" I asked.

"Yes. She came in an hour ago."

"Don't announce me. She expects me," I said. I walked toward the elevators and hesitated. Captain Mullins could get here with a police squad in fifteen or twenty minutes. In much less time than that I would get Kittie out of the fiend's clutches. If not—well, the police might as well capture the murderer.

Stepping into a pay station in the corridor, I called headquarters and asked for Mullins. Fortunately he was in his office and answered almost immediately.

"Peter Hunter, Captain. I have reason to believe that Lita Lawton is in Miss Kittie Ketchum's apartment with Miss Ketchum."

"Coming up!" he cried gleefully.

"Wait a minute," I objected. I explained the note from Kittie, my discovery that the woman was a lightning-change artist, and Williams's deductions. "I'm at the apartment and I'm going upstairs now," I ended.

"You fool!" he shouted. "Wait till I get there. Don't you see it's a trap?"

"What chance would Kittie have if we burst our way in?" I replied. "The woman's mad. There's a chance I can get Kittie away. Lawton doesn't know we're onto her. Good-by."

"Hold on! I'll have men from the precinct station around there in five minutes. I'll be there in fifteen."

"Have your cops surround the building and stop everybody who comes out." I suggested. "By the time you get here it will be all right to break in."

I hung up on his expostulations and took the elevator to the fifth floor. With a beating heart I pressed the button. The door was immediately opened by Kittie—smiling, pretty, and perfectly all right. I heard the piano going in the living room.

"Miss Lawton?" I whispered. "I thought that she was dying?"

"It was a ruse of the poor thing to get me to call on her," Kittie replied. "She's all right, but she has told me the most amazing thing. She wants to talk to you, Peter, and I mean talk."

I had put my gun in the side pocket of my coat where I could keep my hand on it and I held it tight when I walked into the room. The woman I believed to be a brutal murderess rose from the piano and smiled at me in her usual wistful manner. She was dressed as usual. I wondered how she had arrived here without being picked up by the police.

"Miss Lawton isn't dumb," said Kittie. "That's the first surprise."

"I'm sorry it was necessary for me to deceive you about

that," said the woman in a deep, almost masculine voice. "You've been very kind to me, Mr. Hunter. I didn't dare go to your office, but I wanted to talk to you on a matter to our mutual advantage. Please sit down."

I sat down limply. Here I was, nerved up to gunfire, and this was to be a business talk.

"I've made a full confession to Miss Ketchum," Lita Lawton said. "I not only speak, but I sing." She approached me, her eyes very bright. "There never was a singer named Ronald Ray, Mr. Hunter," she said, pausing in front of me. "I was the singer as well as the pianist. That's why we worked in the dark."

"Isn't that amazing?" cried Kittie, much excited.

"Very," I said dryly. "Then you are Ranova?"

She nodded. "Yes. I am Ranova."

"What did you expect to gain by that hocus-pocus?" I demanded.

"I wanted Madame Duplon to hear the voice of which she was so fond—to excite her interest—"

"To engage Ranova for the Perfume program."

"Exactly," she confessed. "I never dreamed that there would be persecution. They broke open my bank vault. It was my money, Mr. Hunter. Of course Ronnie turned everything he earned over to me, and I paid him a salary. He spent every cent of it. I am penniless. I must earn my living." She stretched out her hands imploringly.

"And how do you expect to do it?" I asked.

"That's what I want to talk to you about. This deception was forced on me, Mr. Hunter. I sang years ago and it never got me anything. When Ronnie came to me, I conceived the idea. With his personality and charm and my voice we could become famous. Well, he's gone. I thought that you could announce that it had been a deception, that Lita Lawton, not Ronald Ray, was the world-famous singer. That the public could go right on listening to the voice it loved, and, now that the voice had become celebrated, it wouldn't matter if it came from the throat of a middle-aged spinster instead of a big blond boy."

I stared at her, astounded. If I hadn't know of the letter which had lured Barbara to the Ennis Hotel, I might have been deceived once more.

SURELY NO MORE inoffensive, meek, and pathetic-looking creature ever made an appeal to a man. But she had admitted too much and what she admitted fitted too neatly into the theory I had constructed. She was off guard, obviously unaware that I had anything on her, unconscious that her admission that she was Ranova convinced me that she was the small, weak man who had attacked Barbara with a knife.

"I'd like to talk to you privately," I said. "Kittie, there's an important appointment at the office in a few minutes. You go down there and take care of it. Miss Lawton, this might be put over. It all depends on the way it's presented to the public." What I wanted was to get Kittie out of here before hell broke loose.

"No, no!" Lita Lawton exclaimed. "I want Kittie here. She knows as much about your business as you do."

I measured her. One leap and I could get my hands on her and hold her until Mullins arrived. But I had to get Kittie out of the way.

The phone rang.

"Answer it," snapped the woman. Kittie picked up the instrument.

"Knowlton?" she said. "Why, no. You've the wrong number."

Miss Lawton was opening her handbag. "Let me show you something," she said. Kittie was standing near her and had replaced the receiver on its stand. I was six feet away, sitting on the sofa. And out of the handbag came a small revolver. The woman's face was twisted with fury.

"You treacherous rat!" she snarled and pulled the trigger. Like a flash, Kittie's left arm struck her right arm at the elbow and a bullet drove into the wall above my head. The woman stooped. She thrust her shoulder into Kittie's side, and though Kittie looked larger and stronger, she went down upon the rug.

I was tip and rushing Lita Lawton. She dodged under my arms, darted to the bedroom door, turned, and fired four shots. The flashes blinded me, but the bullets of which went wide. I hesitated, feeling for the automatic which I had forgotten, so suddenly had the situation developed.

The woman darted into the bedroom and closed and locked the door. I drew back to gain momentum for a rush to break it down. A bullet came ripping through the panel of the door. At the same moment Kittie threw her arms around me and held me tight.

"No, no," she cried. "She's mad! You'll be killed!"

"Can she get out of there?" I panted.

"No. There's no other exit. Why did she act like that, Peter? She must be crazy!"

"We've got her!" I exclaimed. "The police will be here in a minute. Kittie, darling, you've been in the hands of a homicidal maniac. I knew it when I came up here. That's why I tried to get you out of the room. By Jove, that phone call was a tip-off! Well, we've got her."

Kittie, who had been hugging me tight, suddenly blushed and released me. "How did you know?" she asked in a scared voice.

Before I could answer came a heavy pounding on the apartment door. Pulling Kittie with me, I ran into the hall and opened up. In streamed Captain Mullins and four plainclothesmen.

"Where is she?" he roared.

"Locked in the bedroom."

He sniffed. "Gunplay? I smell powder."

"She fired six shots that did no damage. She's had time to reload."

"Break down that door," commanded the police captain. A burly patrolman drove with his shoulder at the door. It quivered but held. He drew back and plunged forward once more. The door fell inward and the squad thumped with heavy boots upon it as they rushed the bedroom.

The room was empty. So was the bathroom.

29

WALKING THE PLANK

MULLINS SCOWLED AT me. "What do you mean, she's in there?" he growled.

"She was. Look at the bullet hole in that door panel," I insisted.

"What is she, a magician?" he demanded.

I shrugged my shoulders. "I wouldn't be surprised. She's been everything else."

"Well, she can't vanish into thin air," he retorted, and entering the bedroom, opened a window and thrust his head out. Kittie's apartment was a corner one, and the window looked down upon a side street.

"Hey, Cap, look here," shouted an officer from the bathroom. He had opened the glazed bathroom window. I beat Mullins into the bathroom and we stared incredulously. There was an alley about fifteen feet wide between the back of the apartment hotel and an apartment house on the side street. Directly opposite the bathroom window was a window in the other building, at the same level.

"I suppose she flew over there," sneered Mullins.

But the cop who had been leaning out, withdrew his head.

"There's a plank right below in the alley," he said.

"Couldn't she have walked the plank over to that window', and then knocked the plank away?"

"This is a woman!"

"Mullins," I said. "We found out a lot about her this morning. That woman can do anything."

The captain tore to the telephone. "Tell my men down there," he instructed the operator, "to get around the corner and grab everybody coming out of the apartment house across the alley."

"Come on, men," he said when he hung up. "We'll go through that building with a fine-tooth comb. How much start did she have on us, Hunter?"

"Not more than five minutes."

The police filed out and the door slammed, leaving Kittie and me alone.

"I don't understand it all, Pete," she said faintly. "I'm stunned. Why, you might have been killed."

"Thanks to you I wasn't. Got any notion who you were entertaining? The murderer of Ronnie Ray. The instigator of attempts on my life. The person who first attacked Barbara with a knife and late last night lured her to a hotel room and severely wounded her with that little gun she fired off in here," I said.

Kittie's eyes were so wide they frightened me. All of a sudden she fainted. I caught her before she hit the floor and laid her on her bed. I unfastened her dress at the neck and then I secured a glass of water and sprinkled her face. I didn't know what else to do, but after a few minutes she opened her eyes, smiled at me, and then suddenly rolled over and began to weep bitterly.

I patted her head. "Now, now, it's all over, Kittie."

"It's so horrible," she sobbed. "I—I can't believe it. She used me to get you here to kill you—"

"I don't think so. She actually thought she might persuade me to put her back on the Perfume program. We couldn't have done it if she had been innocent all through, as she supposed I thought."

"But why did she shoot? You said you'd help her!"

I sat down on the bed beside Kittie. "She's not alone in all this, you know," I explained. "She plotted to have you bring her here and she was cunning enough to have everything arranged for a getaway in case I refused to do business with her after she revealed what she supposed I didn't know—that she and not Ronnie was the Singer in the Dark, who used to earn five thousand a week."

"But how did you know?"

"Well, I only found out this morning," I admitted. "In fact, Williams had learned that she was a female baritone."

"Where is Wooster—"

I grinned. "Running round like a hen with its head cut off. He's trying to find you. He thinks a lot of you, Kittie."

Kittie smiled. "He's such a dear."

I didn't like the way she said that much, but I went on talking.

"If I refused to have anything to do with her she intended to shoot us both and escape through your bathroom window. And she had somebody on watch to tip her off if I brought the police with me. You see, Barbara hadn't brought the letter she wrote to the rendezvous, and Lita Lawton wasn't sure it hadn't been found by the police. She was just taking a chance—"

"I don't understand," Kittie repeated.

I then explained to her how Barbara had been induced to go to the Ennis Hotel by a letter much like the one she had received herself. And I reassured her about Barbara's condition, which was improving daily.

"That telephone call asking for somebody named Knowlton was a signal. Somebody down below saw the police enter the building. She realized at once that I planned to capture her, so she pulled the gun. She must have rented the apartment directly opposite yours in the building back there, and the plank was either in place or was pushed across by one of her mob when she opened the bathroom window. She figured, if she killed us both and escaped mysteriously—how did you get her here without the police seeing her?" I demanded suddenly.

"I drove her in my car. She had on a man's coat and a man's hat," Kittie told me.

"Well, if we were dead, she thought she would be safe and then she'd tackle the Duplon's directly. To her diseased mind, getting back on the air is the most important thing in the world, I guess."

Kittie shuddered. "We've had a narrow escape," she said with a sigh. "Peter, you were very brave to come here, knowing what you did."

"Pshaw," I said, embarrassed. "Where did you find her? The police will want the address?"

"In an apartment in Flatbush. Number 863 Ivory Street."

"Of course she won't dare to go back there. Kittie— confound it—"

THE APARTMENT BELL had rung. I went to the door and in walked Wooster Williams. I heard a patter of feet and a door slam as he spoke. Kittie had rolled off the bed and rushed into the bathroom to fix herself—for Williams.

"Big doings, eh?" he said. "Imagine Lita Lawton coming here with Kittie. Is she all right?"

I nodded toward the bathroom.

"Prinking in there," I said. "She recognized your voice. Where the devil were you when all this was going on?"

"I reached headquarters five minutes after Mullins left, was told what you had phoned him, and came up as fast as I could."

"Too late," I sneered. Feeling as I did about Kittie, you can't blame me for being a bit nasty toward Williams.

He lighted one of his preposterous cigars and blew smoke in my face.

"I wouldn't say that," he said blandly. "I nabbed Lita Lawton."

I goggled at him. I was speechless.

"I came up on the subway from headquarters and grabbed a taxi at Lexington and Fifty-ninth," he said. "My driver turned down Park Avenue to duck a red light and was stopped at Park and Fifty-eighth by the lights.

"At that moment, a man reached the corner of Fifty-eighth and Park and turned north. He passed within a few feet of my taxi. He was a small, dark man whose hat was pulled down over his eyes; but what struck me was that he was wearing very small shoes, like a woman's. They weren't high-heeled, but the heels were higher than men wear. And I knew that Lawton had been in Kittie's apartment, a block away. I let him pass, hopped out of the taxi and came up behind him. I had my gun in my right hand and with my left I pulled off his hat. Woman's hair.

" 'Got you, Lita,' I said and placed the muzzle of my gun against the small of her back. She stiffened and fainted. I put her in the taxi and turned her over to Mullins in the lobby downstairs."

"Hello, Wooster," said Kittie from the doorway. She was smiling and self-possessed and looking beautiful. He ran to her and took both her hands. I walked over and looked out the window.

Kittie started telling him excitedly how I had come up here alone, though I was convinced it was a trap.

"Well, I was wrong," I flung over my shoulder. "If I hadn't called the police, and told them to follow me, there wouldn't have been any shooting. I could have kidded that nut and got Kittie clean away."

"If you hadn't come, or if you had brought the police with you," Williams said gravely, "she would have murdered Kittie without a doubt. You did the only thing possible, under the circumstances, and it took plenty of nerve."

"Kittie saved my life," I replied. "Lawton pulled a gun on me and took me completely by surprise. Kittie knocked up her arm when she fired, and that's why I'm cluttering up the atmosphere round here. Take the day off, Kittie. You'll get another reaction. Now that Wooster is here, you don't need me. I've a lot of things to do at the office."

"By all means don't neglect the business," she retorted stiffly. "And I was going to hear a rehearsal of the first Perfume playlet at three o'clock. You'll have to do it."

"Okay." I smiled at them significantly. "The best of luck—to both of you."

Williams had slid in under the wire, I thought bitterly as I rode downtown. I'd fumbled my end. It was bull luck that both Kittie and I hadn't been slain in the fusillade, but along came Williams in the nick of time and grabbed Lita Lawton after she had escaped from the apartment house next door and passed through the cordon of cops.

Of course it was his business to be observant. He was a detective. I wouldn't have looked at a strange man's shoes in a million years. And I knew how he felt about Kittie, and it was pretty obvious how she felt about him. I was due to lose my right arm, which was what she was at the office. I felt pretty miserable, but a man has to carry on.

I called up the hospital and inquired for Barbara when I reached the office. I was told she was better but couldn't see anybody for several days. I ordered a lot of flowers sent up and tried to concentrate on business. It looked like the Ronald Ray mystery was cleared up. There would be no more murders, and I could get rid of the cops who were messing up my apartment. I was back to normalcy.

Mullins called up in about an hour.

"Get a confession out of her?" I asked. He swore viciously.

"I sent her down with two lunkheads," he growled. "Right under their noses, she took poison. She's dead. I thought you ought to know."

After my recent experience I couldn't be horribly sorry.

"Well, it winds the thing up," I said.

"Yeah? How about her pals? How about Ray's double? I was going to squeeze the whole business out of her. And look how she left me."

He sounded so aggrieved that in spite of the tragedy I chuckled.

"Most inconsiderate of her," I said.

"Go to the devil," he snarled, and hung up on me.

Within ten minutes Kittie was on the phone.

"I don't want to be alone, Pete," she said. "Please take me to dinner."

"Where's Wooster?" I asked ungraciously.

"Oh, he had to go. He's going to be awfully busy. That poor woman took poison, but he has to round up her accomplices."

"That's the worst of detectives, they don't keep regular hours," I said.

"Are you taking me to dinner or aren't you?"

"I most certainly am. Call for you at six," I surrendered.

"Couldn't you come at five? I'm very nervous. And Peter, Wooster says you must still take precautions—you're not out of danger."

"The heck with Wooster! See you at five," I said.

"Oh, very well," she said, laughing. "Good-by, Peter."

30

THE DOUBLE

I WAS PREPARING to leave, at four-thirty, when the young man who was solicitous for my welfare but who had the inside track with the only girl I would ever love, phoned in.

"How are you, Hunter?" Williams inquired. "I'm calling from Millford."

"What on earth are you doing up there?"

"I want you to hop right up here and identify a body."

"What's that?" I shouted. "I'm not identifying any more bodies, thank you!"

"Sorry, but you'll have to. About one o'clock this afternoon the state police found a body sunk in the swamp near where Miss Bond was confined. Bullet wound in the back of the head. Answers to the description of Ronald Ray."

"The double!" I exclaimed.

"Yes, or Ray himself. How soon can you get here?"

"How long has he been dead? Of course it's not Ronnie," I insisted.

"Well, you're the one who can best say. He's been dead a week or more."

I shuddered. "I can't make it until late tonight. He can wait a few hours longer."

"I'm sorry, you must come immediately. If you refuse, I'll ask headquarters to bring you up."

"All right, confound you," I said sullenly.

"I'm leaving immediately. Got a clue," Williams went on. "You'll find the body at the undertaker's in Millford. You'll find Sergeant Brewster of the state police at the station house and he'll take you over. Will expect you in an hour or an hour and a half, eh?"

"I suppose so. Say, Williams, when this business is finally settled, consider our acquaintance at an end, will you?" I said nastily.

I heard him laugh. "Delighted," he replied. "It isn't as if I was fond of you, Hunter."

I phoned Kittie the bad news and ordered out my car. For the third time I drove out of New York to the sinister little town of Millford. At six I stopped before the small frame building labeled "Police Station," and found a burly but agreeable state police sergeant sitting there chatting with the local talent. I introduced myself and we walked across the street to an undertaker's shop.

The undertaker, a greasy little man, led us into the back room.

"The body's in bad condition," he warned, and lifted a sheet from a long, gruesome object. I turned sick and backed away after a glance.

"I can't tell," I said faintly. "Bears a general resemblance, in size and the shape of the head, to Ray."

"But you wouldn't swear it was he?"

"You got to get used to things like that," said the sergeant sympathetically. "Take a swig of this."

I swallowed some bad whisky; choked, but felt better.

He took my arm and led me back to the police station. "Give me that report," he requested of the Millford officer in charge. "Mr. Hunter, this is the medical examiner's description of the body."

This was easier. I ran my eye down the doctor's specifications. Hair, color of eyes, height, weight were about like Ronnie's. There was a two-tooth bridge on the lower jaw, right.

"Not Ronald Ray," I said. "Of course, it couldn't be. Ray's teeth were perfect. He told me himself he never had to have dentistry. And the teeth of the body in New Jersey were perfect. This is the double."

"I figured it was," said the sergeant. "After Miss Bond made her getaway, they must have decided they didn't need this stooge any more so they snuck up on him and put a slug in his brain."

"Can I go now?" I asked.

"Just sign the statement about the bridgework, proving it isn't Ronald Ray."

I filled out a form and signed it. The sergeant and the local officer signed as witnesses, and with great relief I stepped into my car and rolled out of Millford for what I hoped was the last time.

ABOUT A QUARTER past eight I parked in front of Kittie's apartment house and asked the operator to call her. I thought it likely that Kittie might have had her dinner sent up to her room.

"Oh, Miss Ketchum went out about six-thirty," she said.

"Alone?"

"No, there was a gentleman with her. A friend of hers named Mr. Williams."

"Thanks," I said. I turned quickly so the operator couldn't see how red my face got. Of all the contemptible tricks. But no. I had to be fair. It wasn't a trick, really. I had to make the trip to Millford to identify Ray's double, and Williams, having been on the job up there, had finished and followed his clue, if he had one, back to New York. And it was natural, since he had to eat, to call up Kittie and inquire if she would dine with him.

Nevertheless, I got the worst of the deal. As far as Kittie was concerned, I'd continue to run second to the Federal agent, confound him. So I went into a bar and lifted several. I had more to drink than was good for me at dinner and I went home about ten o'clock, dizzy but not happy. I was dour.

And after I'd gone to bed, instead of sleeping, I lay awake thinking about how a small, dowdy, meek-looking piano player like Lita Lawton could have been a devil in human form. For the murder of the unfortunate who looked like Ronald Ray must be charged to her door, like the other crimes. Either Lawton or one of her accomplices had discovered this fellow and hired him or terrorized him into participation in the kidnaping of Barbara.

She was dead, like her victims; but there were a lot of things yet to be cleared up by Williams and the police. There was the man who had starved Barbara for three days to force her into signing checks. There were at least four men, including Ronnie's double, on the Bear Mountain Road where Barbara had been captured and I had had a narrow escape from death. If these miscreants could be run down we might learn why they took orders from a crazy woman, and the secret of Ronnie's strange death, which was about as mysterious as ever.

And with what the authorities now had to go on, rounding up the survivors of the gang shouldn't be impossible.

31

A GIRL HATES TO EAT ALONE

KITTIE WAS AT her desk when I reached the agency in the morning. She looked fresh as a rose and gave me a nod when I stopped to speak to her. "I'm up to my neck, right now," she said. "I'll be in your office in ten minutes."

When she came in she brought her notebook, but I hadn't looked at my mail. I was just sitting there thinking what a fool I'd been to have this jewel so close to me for years and not appreciate her properly until it was too late.

"I'm sorry about last night," I said.

"I understood. I was sorry for you. It must have been a dreadful experience."

"It was. I'm glad you didn't have to dine alone."

She lifted her very nice eyebrows. "Oh, you know that?"

"I called at your place at eight. No doubt Williams was better company."

She laughed a little. "Wooster is really a lot of fun."

"No doubt," I snapped.

"We just had dinner and he left me at my place. He had a hot trail to follow, he said."

"Yeah? It had chance to get cold while you were dining and dancing."

She looked sort of dreamy. "He's really a lovely dancer."

"Aw, come back later," I growled. "I haven't read my letters yet."

"Very well," she said demurely, and went off.

A couple of days went by without incident or excitement. Williams didn't show his nose around the office and the police let me alone. With Lita Lawton out of the way I ought to be able to get things well organized again, instead of spinning plots like a black widow spider.

Kittie, though, was acting queer—sort of formal. She didn't call me Pete and she didn't bawl me out in her funny way. She was strictly business. I figured she was having dinner with Williams every night. That bothered me a lot, but I wouldn't demean myself to ask if she were seeing him.

About three o'clock on the third afternoon she came in. She had a glint in her eyes.

"Look here, Peter," she said sharply, "what's the matter with you?"

"Nothing. Why?"

"You've been acting as though I were poison."

"Who? Me?"

"Yes, you. You haven't taken me to lunch or dinner for three days."

"I figured you were heavily dated," I said sullenly.

"Indeed! Well, I've dined alone, since the night you went to Millford. Wooster has been awfully busy."

"He must have been," I said.

"If there was any hope you'd be good company, I'd ask you to take me stepping tonight," she suggested.

"It's a date, though I don't expect I'll be as much fun as Mr. Williams."

"You make me weary," she retorted as she moved toward her office. "Six-thirty."

"I can make it. I'm going up to see Barbara at five. Her nurse said she's well enough to see people and wants to talk to me. She wants to have you call on her, too."

"That's fine. I'll go tomorrow. Be seeing you."

KITTIE HAD ON a black evening dress and wore over it a white fur jacket that couldn't have been very warm, for it only fell to her waist. Her hair was fluffed and awfully pretty. I'd never seen her so dolled up.

"I want to celebrate the end of all this horror," she said when we started out. "I'd like to get out of my mind, if I can, the way that dreadful woman looked when she drew the revolver from her handbag and pointed it at you. And to forget the way she killed Ronnie. And wounded Barbara."

"Best suggestion I can make is drinks," I answered. "Though I've tried 'em myself and they don't do much good. Waldorf bar, first."

We went round to a couple of hotel bars and finally arrived for dinner in a restaurant with the tables in terraces around a dance floor, with shaded lights and semi-privacy. Thanks to looking at Kittie and having had cocktails, my spirits were better than they had been for days. Of course I knew I was pinch-hitting for Wooster Williams, but Kittie was all the more bewitching because she was out of my reach.

We'd got along to the coffee when Kittie put her elbows on the table and cupped her chin in her palm and gazed at me hard.

"You're going to propose to Barbara soon," she said. "Or have you?"

"I have not," I said indignantly.

She smiled brightly. "Now is your time. When one is ill in a hospital, one's resistance is weak. And if it wasn't, she'd have you. She never loved Ronnie, you know. That was an infatuation induced by Lita Lawton's voice. I was crazy about him myself, and so were thousands of women. Barbara's had you marked for slaughter since the night she took you riding to Bear Mountain. There's a woman who always gets her man."

"Barbara is a swell girl," I said. "Beautiful. About the most remarkable girl I ever met, but I have no intention of becoming Mr. Barbara Bond, Miss Ketchum."

"Pete, that's nasty!"

I chuckled. "Besides, I'm in the discard. Do you know what she told me this afternoon?"

"What?"

"That she's mad about Dr. Oldham, who's attending her. She said that she's going to propose to him the first time she can penetrate through his professional manner."

"That was just feeling you out," Kittie remarked.

"Was it? This doctor is a big, strapping, handsome young fellow. He came in when I was there and I could see by the way they looked at each other that they're both sunk."

"Poor Pete," sighed Kittie. "I'm so sorry."

"You should be sorry, but not on account of her. I'm not a guy who can be dragged around like a dog on a leash. That night she drove up to Bear Mountain my hair would have turned white if it hadn't turned already. I was sort of goofy about her, but her driving cured me. Even when I brought her home from Millford, the feeling didn't come back. When I marry, Miss Ketchum, I'm going to be the boss."

"And your wife won't be able to say that her soul is her own," she said sadly. "How terrible."

"I mean my wife and I will be partners... shucks, I'm never going to get married. I suppose you're walking out on the Hunter Agency pretty soon?"

"Who can tell?" inquired Kittie lightly. "I suppose, though, it would be a good idea to reduce the staff."

"Eh?"

"I think I could go to the Upshaw Agency. They've hinted a few times."

"Quit your kidding. You're going to marry this swell-headed detective."

"Wooster is not swell-headed!" she snapped at me. "Having a very youthful appearance, he had to strut a little, but he really is a very sweet boy."

"Has he proposed yet?"

Kittie nodded solemnly.

"Then what the deuce are you talking about the Upshaw Agency for?"

"A girl has to have a job. Wooster asked me to marry him the night you went to Millford. I said I liked him awfully but I wasn't in love with him. That's why I haven't seen him since, I suppose."

"Oh!" I exclaimed. I stared at her. "You're too hard-boiled to love anybody," I said sullenly.

KITTIE'S EYES GREW dark and her mouth set in a straight line. "I'd like to sock you right in the nose for that crack," she said furiously. "I wish we were somewhere alone so I could use my claws on you."

"Yeah.... Want to dance?"

"No!"

We sat there in strained silence for a few minutes.

"Peter," she said in a very different tone. "I'm sorry. A girl has to act hard-boiled in business. I forgot what you did the other day. You knew exactly what you were stepping into when you came to my apartment. You must have thought a lot of me."

"Of course I thought a lot of you."

"Peter," said Kittie, "you acted—when I fainted—I could have killed Wooster Williams for coming in when he did."

I grasped the edge of the table. Kittie's eyes were brimming.

"Look here!" I said sharply. "I was just going to kiss you when he came in."

Kittie's smile was positively dazzling. "Don't I know it?" she asked softly.

"Say, by any possibility, do you think of me in any way except as a big, noisy, thick-headed, four-flushing advertising agent?"

"Do you think of me in any way except as a hard-boiled, efficient office worker?" she countered.

Oh, boy, oh, boy, did I feel good! I grinned. "Match you to see which answers first."

"We've matched and you lost," she said tensely.

I gulped. I was red as a tomato. Boy, it was hard to tell that little slangy mutt that I thought she was the loveliest, most beautiful and finest girl in the world. I did, though— think so, I mean.

"You poor ape," said Kittie scornfully, "when you've had all the encouragement in the world, can't you say, 'I love you'?"

"Well, I do, damn it!" I ejaculated.

Kittie sighed. "So that's that. Like pulling one of your teeth. And I had to break the heart of a lovely boy to make you realize that I was worth looking at."

"I knew it all the time!" I exclaimed.

"Skip that. Gosh, Pete, I was scared to death that Barbara would grab you and turn you into Joe Penner's duck. Take me home."

"Can I come in with you?"

"You bet your life you're coming in," said Kittie fiercely. "Oh, Pete, I want to cry."

I choked. "Darn it, so do I," I said thickly.

32

FLASH OF DEATH

A LONG ABOUT two A.M. I arrived at my apartment and to my astonishment, Wooster Williams was sitting there playing blackjack with Watts, who had the dog watch.

"Hello, Peter," he said cheerfully. "You and Kittie make a night of it?"

"Know everything, don't you?" I said with a grin. I didn't hate him any more. I was sorry for him.

"You bet. You and Kittie fixed it all up, eh?"

"Say, you're incredible," I gasped.

He laughed cheerfully. "It's written on your pan. Besides she told me the other night she'd been goofy about you for years. Well, I'm a fellow who has no right to get married. Likely to be bumped off at any minute. Watts, you can go home. The chief told me to tell you to when I came in, but I needed company—"

"Oh, well," replied the cop. "Hunter's liquor is prime. I kind of liked this job."

"Thought you said I had to be careful," I said to Williams.

"Case is closed, Hunter," Williams informed me. "At eight tonight we nabbed a character known as Billy the Bronx Bum. He used to be a bootlegger and then a rack-eteer, but things got too hot and he was wondering where

his next thousand dollars were coming from a few weeks
ago."

"Didn't Sergeant Caffery say that Louie the Loup used
to do jobs for him?"

Williams nodded. He yawned. "I'm awfully tired. Big
night. How about putting me up?"

"You bet," I said enthusiastically. Wooster certainly was
a swell guy.

"Billy's last name was Higgins," he said with another
yawn. "Tough egg."

I sat down and poured myself a drink. "Stop grand-
standing," I told him. "You're all swelled up and you came
up here to do a little gloating. How does the Bronx Bum
come into the picture?"

"His real name is Donald Warren," he said. "Brother of
Alice Warren, if you follow me. They come of a good family
in Hackettstown, New Jersey."

"Hackettstown? Why, that's near—"

"The inn where you found Ray's body," he said, smiling.
"One of the suspects the police picked up near Millford
after Barbara's escape was a man named Anderson. They
had nothing on him and had to let him go, but Captain
Mullins put a man on his trail. He used to drive a beer
truck for Billy the Bronx Bum. They've been trying since
to tie up Billy with Anderson's presence near Millford.

"In the breast pocket of the vest of Ray's double was a
manila envelope torn open. It looked as though a check or
a big bill in it had been removed. There was blood on the
envelope, and plainly marked in blood was the print of a
forefinger on one side and a thumb on the other. I rushed

it up to police headquarters here. That's why I couldn't wait for you in Millford.

"They compared Anderson's fingerprints—they had them. Didn't match. And then they tried Billy's. They were the same. So Billy killed the poor devil who was found in the swamp. His coat was tightly buttoned, so the envelope was in good shape and landed the murderer for us.

"We caught Billy eating supper tonight in his apartment in the Bronx. He blustered and protested, but we yanked him down town. He's a big, tough fellow, and he held out a long time under the lights, but we had him cold and he knew it, and finally he told everything. Gosh, I'm tired."

"Quit acting," I said. "You hung round here until I came home to tell me this."

"Well, maybe I did. You had a poor opinion of me as a detective, but I've solved this case.

"Billy hadn't seen his sister for years and got a cold reception when he called on her after she and Ronnie got into the papers. He threatened to expose her graft. Of course he knew that she had a man's singing voice. She paid him ten thousand dollars and stopped his mouth.

"The day the engagement of Ronnie to Barbara was announced Lita sought him out. He says she claimed that Ray had wronged her and was now, not only jilting her, but ruining their business because Miss Bond was sure to find out he couldn't sing. They talked it over and finally hit on a scheme.

"Billy was to pose as a guard from the Indiana State Penitentiary who had recognized Ray. He called him on the phone and demanded a hundred thousand dollars. The money must be paid in cash at four in the morning in this inn beyond Dover, New Jersey.

"Ray, of course, was turning his money over to Lita. So in great distress, he went to her and told her of the demand. She immediately agreed to put up the money and to go with him to the rendezvous. They would start from her apartment in her car. After he left Barbara that night he went there instead of back to his hotel.

"THEY DROVE DOWN to the inn. The door had been unboarded and unlocked, but the place was dark. A voice called to come upstairs. Ray hung back.

" 'Don't be frightened,' Lita Lawton said. 'All he wants is money, and being a prison guard, he's terrified he'll be caught dealing with an ex-convict.'

"So Ronnie Ray went up the stairs and into a lighted room where Billy the Bum was waiting for him.

" 'Sit down,' he said, pointing to a chair by the window. 'Bring the money?'

" 'Yes,' said Lita.

" 'I told you to come alone—'

" 'I handle all his business affairs,' Lita stated. 'Sit down, Ronnie. Everything is going to be all right.'

"Outside there was a storm and thunder and lightning. Ray sat down. A man came out from behind, unseen by him, stepped up behind the chair, and deftly twisted a rope around his body, making him fast. 'Take hold of this wire,' commanded Billy. He thrust into Ronnie's hands a copper wire which came in through the window behind.

" 'Now, Lita,' said Billy. 'Do your stuff.'

"He claims he and Anderson—that was the other

fellow—stepped out into the hall but he heard what his sister said.

"She stepped up in front of Ray and shook her fist in his face.

" 'I've got you,' she screamed. 'You'd ditch me, would you, and marry that baby-faced blonde? After all I've done for you!'

" 'So this was a plot,' Ronnie answered. 'Well, Lita, you could send me back to prison, but you won't because you're insane about money and you'd lose my radio salary. I'm going to marry Barbara but I'll go right on working with you. Don't worry about my giving myself away to Barbara.'

" 'Take hold of that wire,' she commanded. Billy said she drew a pistol. 'You're a deceiver and a traitor. I made you, and I'll finish you. If you don't swear that you'll break your engagement, I'll turn on the juice and electrocute you like the skunk you are. You're killing me. I love you so—'

"There came a tremendous flash of lightning, a deafening peal of thunder, and Billy heard Lita scream horribly. He ran into the room. Ronnie's head had fallen on his breast, and his hands clutched the wire tightly."

"She turned on the juice!" I exclaimed.

Wooster Williams shook his head.

"Billy swears that the wire was only five or six feet long and its other end was held down by the window sill. It wasn't connected with anything. But Ronnie had been electrocuted, just the same, by a stroke of lightning," Williams said.

"Do you think it true?" I gasped.

"Those are high voltage wires which pass over the inn. Billy and Anderson claim they don't know anything about electricity—that there was no intention of killing Ray. All Billy wanted was the hundred thousand, half of which he had agreed to give back to Lita. The police have no record that either of them were electricians. Billy says she expected to scare Ronnie into breaking the engagement with Barbara.

"Anyway, the three of them ran down the stairs in a panic. Lita fainted and they carried her out. They then boarded up the door, jumped into their car and drove back to New York as fast as they could."

"I believe that," I declared. "Do you?"

"I'm inclined to," Williams nodded. "They knew they ought to dispose of the body, but nothing would induce any of them to go near the inn again. They hoped that the body wouldn't be discovered for a couple of month's, which would give them time to get under cover.

"Well, they laid low for a couple of weeks—at least Billy did. Lita, of course, had to show herself at the broadcast that night and remain where she could be questioned for a few days. She was so griefstricken and terrified that she seemed harmless.

"About a couple of weeks later, Billy bumped into a clerk in a Bronx store named Herbert Sanders who was a dead ringer for Ronnie Ray. It gave him an idea. He hired the fellow without telling him what he was wanted for. He got in touch with Lita. He wanted to get a ransom out of Barbara Bond. By this time Lita had concentrated her hate on you and Barbara, and held you two responsible for the death of the man she loved. She agreed, but insisted that Barbara be held for ransom after she had paid the ransom for Ronnie, which was all right with her brother.

"With her voice and Sanders' resemblance to Ronnie, it looked like a cinch. We know that her real motive was to murder Barbara, her rival. Billy claims not to have known that, at the time. They called Barbara up. Ronnie's voice sang to her. They set the rendezvous outside Dover because Billy and Lita were brought up in that territory and knew every byroad.

"Well, Barbara lost her nerve and made a getaway, while you and Kittie, following her, went down a side road and blundered into the inn and found Ronnie. It looked like this spoiled their plans and Lita's wrath against you was intensified because your discovery seemed to have balked them. She paid her brother to have you put out of the way. He sent Louie first, and then Anderson. Anderson knifed Forman—not knowing what you looked like. At least, Billy charges him with that crime.

"LITA WAS DELIGHTED to have you accompany Barbara on the second expedition. You were to be shot out of hand, but you escaped them. Your escape, after seeing Ronnie's double, made her plan to go back on the radio with the new Ronnie hopeless. And Sanders was scared to death at the business he found himself in. He was getting troublesome.

"It was decided to put him out of the way. Billy and Anderson took him away from the cottage in a car that night, shot him and dumped him in the swamp. And Lawton, in a burst of insane rage, double-crossed her brother by taking advantage of his absence to try to murder Barbara. When Billy came back and found she had escaped, he and Lita jumped in their car and made for New York. Anderson, who was still in the swamp, had to make his getaway on foot and was picked up by a state policeman along with other persons who couldn't give a good account of their presence in that vicinity.

"Now, for two years Lita had been making use of the Ranova personality for income tax evasion. She had a safety deposit box in Ranova's name and, with the double out of the way, she made the desperate effort to get back into radio on her own. She had paid off her brother. She sent the poisoned whisky to you herself. At least, he claims to know nothing about it. With Ranova exposed, she persisted in her crazy ambition and that's why she had you come to Kittie's apartment. Now can I go to bed?"

"Why didn't the police discover that the electric wire wasn't connected with the high voltage lines?" I asked.

"They supposed the connection had been removed and the wire cut off so that no attention would be attracted."

I drew a long breath. "All right," I said. "Let's go to bed. But if you think I'll sleep—"

"I should worry if you sleep. I know I will," Williams said.

I HAD A talk a few days later with a big psychologist who was much interested in Lita Lawton and who came in to ask me some questions about her.

"She wasn't insane in the technical sense," he told me. "I would say she had a fixation. I'm certain that there was no desire on her part to kill Ray. She had a double reason for wanting him to live, she loved him, and she needed him in her business. When he was struck by lightning something snapped in her brain. She wanted revenge. Absolving herself like all egotists, she sought for someone to blame for his death and decided that the woman to whom he was engaged, and the man who had brought the pair together—you—were his murderers.

He went into a lot of detail regarding obsessions, fixations and forms of mania that bored me. But his deductions seemed reasonable.

Well, the Ranova money is still in the bank, while obscure relatives of Lita Lawton and Ralph Ray, Ronnie's worthless cousin, are fighting for the balance above the two hundred thousand, which was returned to Barbara.

Kittie and I went down to the City Hall and got a marriage license, stood up before a preacher and took a week's cruise to Bermuda for our honeymoon.

The publicity that came to me didn't do any harm. On the contrary it brought me new clients and my business is pretty good. Kittie absolutely refuses to stay home and run a house so we live in an apartment with service, go downtown together, run the shop and ride home together and play married couple in the evenings—which is pretty nice, I can tell you.

Barbara came through with a magnificent silver service for a wedding present, and a few days later announced her engagement to the doctor.

Just at present she is making arrangements for a round-the-world solo flight. I've taken a motor ride with Barbara once, and I bet she breaks all records.